©A family love affair

A love story full of intrigue,
jealousy, hate, conspiracy
murder, and honesty

This story is a work of fiction. Names,
characters, organizations, places and
events are either the product of the
author imagination or are used
fictitiously. Any resemblance
to persons living or dead
are entirely coincidental

Published by Amazon 2022

A family love affair

by

Giuliano Laffranchi

Introduction

Summertime is approaching fast in Greatstone a lovely little town in the South of England, situated non far from the sea, it has all the amenities and nice things for the residents to enjoy, and yes, it has a beautiful theatre, a couple of cinemas, and a very big garden in the middle of the town, which host the various entertainments, and of course, the yearly visit from the well known Clowny Circus.

Edward Collins, Eddy to his friends and mum Claire, have a daughter, Suzanne, they simply adore her, not because she's beautiful, maybe because she's the only child, but even so, she's not spoiled, the family is all exited as in a few weeks she will be eighteen years old, and for that big day they promised her a holiday on the Italian Riviera, at the same time they'll have a chance to visit uncle John, who is now working as a General Manager in a five stars Hotel.

Dad Eddy is an experienced car mechanic working for Jack Mellin a local garage owner and mum Claire is a part-timer for a local solicitor, their earnings are not great but they can cope alright, luckily they live in a semidetached house with a lovely garden, inherited by Clair late parents. Suzanne works for a local hairdresser, doing rather well and making quite a few extra pounds from generous ladies customers. All summoned up they are quite a happy family.

Chapter 1

"Hello darling…I'm in, where are you?"

"Oh, hello Eddy… I'm in the kitchen, I'm just finishing this pie, just about to go in the oven… Bytheway your brother John rung this morning from Italy as you went off to work….How was your day?"

"Not too bad darling, quite unfortunate really, a customer brought his car back as he wasn't very happy with my service… Incidentally what did he say John?"

"I'll tell all about it you later Eddy….What was wrong with that customer then?"

"Nothing much really, to be quite honest, his car is so flipping old, that it really needs a new engine!"

"I see what you mean Eddy, you should have told your boss."

"Well, Jack knows that but he's afraid of losing a customer, by telling that fellow his problem, in saying that, he managed to convince him that a car don't last forever, unless of course, some new parts are replaced, and that would have cost him a packet!"

"That is a nice way of dealing Eddy, I'm sure Jack was able to put his mind at rest!"

"True Claire, the chap looked quite worried, went in his car and said to Jack, to keep his eye on some second hand cars, and he will be willing to get rid of his old banger!"

"I'm sure that settled the unpleasant situation!"

"Yes, that did it! I say…. Suzanne seem to be a bit late tonight, don't you think so?"

"Don't worry darling, it's only late by ten minutes!"

"Speak of the devil Julia, just heard the door opening!"

"That would be Suzanne, dinner will be ready in half an hour Eddy."

"Hello mum, hello dad....Oh what a very pleasant day I had!"

"Oh… you are lucky sweetheart!"

"Why…Did you have a bad day dad?"

"Never mind darling, it's not all that important!"

"Yes darling dad is right, just go and have wash dinner will be ready in a few minutes, as we must discuss our holiday trip to the Italian Riviera."

"Jolly good mum, did you hear from uncle John then?"

"Yes darling he rung this morning as you and dad left for work.

"Oh, I just can't wait to hear what he had to say, and what kind of place he found for us!"

"Go on darling, off you go upstairs, by the time you come down the dinner will be on the table!"

Suzanne uncle…Thirty years old John Collins is divorced from Gloria a high society rich English lady, they had no children so the split went off easy and he's quite happy to live his life as a flamboyant distinctive English gentleman in this classy hotel on the Italian Riviera, he knows his job alright and how to charm the ladies, unlike his brother Eddy who loves his wife very much and is daughter Suzanne, he enjoy his job as a mechanic, therefore his profession never gave him the taste of wealth like his brother had, never the less he's happy.

(The two brothers always keep in touch, although Eddy never took financial advantages from brother John, that is when he was swimming in money and probably now too, he's the sort of man that enjoys married life routine and likes to be independent. But John always had more money than he needed. Now he has asked his brother and family to visit him in Italy, of course he can't accommodate them in the hotel where he works, but he offered to find them a suitable accommodation in a hotel nearby. Eddy thought that was a good idea, for the shear fact that Suzanne was soon to be eighteen years old and that is supposed to be her birthday present he accepted John's offer, provided John doesn't pay for it, which was verbally agreed between the two)

"This pie is superb Claire, sometimes I just don't know how you can manage to work those long hours and produce something like this!"

"Thank you darling, there's plenty more, please help yourself!"

"I'll have a couple of spoonful more mum, if you don't mind.."

"There you are my love, it's so nice to see you so healthy and with good appetite."

"She's a big girl now Claire, in fact I think you should have half glass of this wine, it's not very dry, in fact it's rather mellow….here darling, try it!"

"Thanks dad, I will, but to be honest I'm not a wine drinker, I do enjoy soft drinks!"

"Don't you give her bad habits father Eddy, she's got plenty of time to get around that kind of taste!"

"Oh….Alright Claire, that won't hurt her…."

"Hey you two… please don't argue on my account, if you don't mind let us talk about uncle John, I really miss him, he's always so nice to me, he treats me like his own daughter!"

"Oh yes darling, he rung this morning and he told me that he managed to find a very nice and modest hotel for us, almost attached to where he works, it's not very expensive, he said he won't cost more than two hundred euro a day for the three of us, including food, I thought that was not too bad, One thousand eight hundred euro for the three of us!"

"That is fantastic mum….Oh…I'm looking so forward to see him, and to see where he works, it must be a very high class hotel, according to the photos!"

"Oh yes Suzanne it is a five stars place, I can assume a lot of very rich people uses that!"

"No doubt you are right Eddy….Well… he said to let him know the date of our arrival, and he'll do the rest."

"Wonderful Claire, tomorrow I'll have a chat with Jack, and see if I can have three weeks off!"

"Why three weeks Eddy?"

"Well, if are going by car, we'll have to stay for two weeks, then of course we shall have the opportunity to visit some other places."

"That'll be nice Eddy, in fact John mentioned that our hotel has parking spaces too."

"That is wonderful dad, I'll have to start looking around for some swimming costumes!"

"I might as well join you darling, tomorrow is Saturday we shall visit that big store that opened last week!"

"And they say it's not very expensive mum!"

"Don't start cutting corners Suzanne, I shall treat you both to some good stuff."

"Goodness me, can I have that in writing Eddy?"

"Are sure dad? You are feeling alright....I hope!"

"Oh... you are so funny you two, can I have some pudding please, on second thoughts I think I shall have a couple of slices of that Italian ice cream you bought last week!"

"That is called the cassata dad..."

"Whatever is, I did like it the other day!"

"I'll have some of that too mum, then if you join me, there's a good film on the telly!"

"Of course darling as it is my turn to wash up tonight!"

"Oh mum...I'll do it if you like."

"Don't worry darling, you just go and sit yourself with your daddy!"

"Thank you mum, but tomorrow will be my turn!"

"Don't worry darling, you'll do enough washing during your married life!"

"Please don't rush me to the alter mother, I don't even have a boyfriend for that matter."

"You'll soon be there girl, before you know it!"

"Here mum, come and have a look at this...."

"It's nothing new darling, your dad usually goes off to sleep after dinner, in fact all my friends say that, I guess he's relaxing, then of course he had a couple of glasses of wine, he's not used to that a lot, but I like to treat him to a good bottle now and then!"

"I think I shall go and watch the film in my bedroom mum, if you don't mind!"

"You do as you please, but don't stay up too long, as I would like to go shopping early tomorrow morning.!

"Oh....Hello sleeping beauty.....Now you are too late to watch that lovely film, because it just finished, I'm sure Suzanne watched it up stairs in her bedroom, she's quite a fan of that Billy Johnson, really good looking chap!"

"Goodness me Claire, you fancy him too? I seemed to have fallen asleep, I really wanted to watch that film!"

"I'm sure you did, tell you something Eddy, you sat in that chair and you went off like a log."

"Sorry darling, maybe I felt a bit tired, still I'm going to watch the news now, and then I'll hit the sack.!

"Please yourself darling, I'm going up now, and you.... don't be late, you'll have to work all day tomorrow, although is Saturday."

"I've got the message love, I won't be long...You know one thing that came to my mind while I was relaxing!"

"What is it Eddy?"

"Well I was thinking about my parents, you know they haven't seen my brother John for quite a few years and I was wondering...."

"No way Eddy, this is supposed to be a very special holiday for us two and Susanna, if we start thinking to take your parents it won't be the same, further more they are not young as they used to be, therefore travelling by car it would exhausting for them!"

"I think you have a good point there Claire, so forget I even mention it!"

"Glad you mentioned it, because tomorrow we shall pay them a visit, and I will personally tell them that we are going to Italy, and see their reaction!"

"Please do that Claire, I'm sure they'll be pleased!"

"So glad that you agree with me Eddy, and please don't be late.... goodnight darling!"

"Goodnight Claire...."

Chapter 2

"Breakfast is ready Susanne and will you tell your dad, I think he's in the shower."

"Okay mum…I won't be long!"

"Here Susanna, a nice boiled egg and toasted soldiers, just like the school days and a nice cuppa!"

"Thank you mum, yes I do love this, god knows how many eggs I had so far, that is since I was a kid."

"Ah, ah, ah, I guess thousands, maybe you should have kept a diary, remember how much I tried to make you eat cereals, but you always refused?"

"Yes I do mum, I still don't like them."

"Good morning young ladies, what was that about cereals?"

"Nothing darling, here you fried egg and bacon, and two slices of toast, that might keep you going till lunch time."

"Thank you love, don't put too much in the lunch box."

"Don't worry, I put a couple of apples with your ham sandwiches."

"That'll be lovely darling, many thanks, Jack always fills me up with tea and coffee, that man is really a nice fellow, I couldn't be treated better."

"Well you worked long enough for him, so he should, how many years?"

"Well… since I left school I'd say."

"And please don't forget to ask Jack for some dates, and make sure to make that special one in the middle of the three weeks then this evening we shall ring John to book us that hotel."

"Right Oh…all recorded…"

"That's good, all settled then..I'm going up to get ready Susanna, and then we shall go and some window shopping!"

"Oh you are generous mum!"

"Bye, bye young ladies and please don't spend too much, remember we have that expensive holiday coming up!"

"There he goes again mum….Mr. Scrooge!"

"Ah, ah, ah, ah….Have a nice day…."

"Good morning Jack, how are you today?"

"I'm fine thank you, but I must tell you I didn't sleep well last night!"

"Is that so, unlike myself, after dinner I fell asleep on my special armchair, I woke up when the film I planned to watch ended, thereafter my darling sent me up to bed, and I slept like a log."

"You lucky old devil…you!"

"Well, I suppose I am in a way, I try to avoid the problems I haven't got!"

"I wish I could do that Eddy, you know business hasn't been too bad, but the overheads are over taking my financial situation, still I shouldn't complain, I've got no others to feed!"

"I'm sorry to hear that, actually I am surprise, by the look of our number of customers, I always thought that you wouldn't have any problems as such!"

"It's true Eddy, but as I said it's the overheads, and of course don't forget that we have quite a competition with the other lot!"

"You mean the other garages?"

"That's alright my friend, in fact I'm seriously thinking of retire while the sun is shining!"

"You mean you would sell the business, goodness me, you are scaring me Jack, where would I find a job like this?"

"Don't you start worrying Eddy, if I ever would think to sell this business, you would be the first one to know, rest assure of that, don't worry!"

"That's very thoughtful of you Jack, but I don't think I could never afford to buy you out!"

"Don't be silly Eddy, there are many ways that a switch over can be done, after all you know all our regulars, and you know exactly how to treat them."

"You've got a point there Jack, but before we can go further with his conversation, there's one thing I want to ask you!"

"Spit out Eddy, I am all ears!"

"As you know we always close down for a couple of weeks every year, for our holidays…."

"That's true Eddy, and what do you suggest?"

"Well, this year is the eighteen birthday of my darling Susanne, and Claire and I were thinking to give her a good present by taking her on holiday to Italy, at the same time we would pay a visit to my brother John and…"

"My wife and could do with a longer holiday too!"

"That's alright then Jack, why don't you take three weeks too?"

"Yes you are right….That is fantastic Eddy.. when were you thinking to take this holiday then?"

"Her birthday is the fifteen of July, we would like to go a week before, then we could celebrate the happy event in Italy, but of course the problem is that we are going by car, and therefore I shall need to take three weeks instead of the usual two."

"I don't see any problems about that Eddy, in fact instead of closing for two weeks we shall close for three, how's does it sounds to you?"

"But…that is marvelous Jack, it couldn't be better!"

"So that's it then Eddy, we shall close a weeks before the 15th and open three weeks later, so I can have three weeks off for myself and my darling Doreen!"

"Will you go somewhere too Jack?"

"Yes, I think we might go to Glasgow to see my dear sister, whom I haven't seen for donkeys' years/"

"That's a good Idea Jack, now then enough of this, let me get on with some work, which is the first problem?"

"That old banger over there, it needs the oil change, and please check the breaks!"

"That's no problem Jack."

(In the meantime Claire and Susanne arrived at their local shopping centre.)

"Oh…I like this mum, but…..I think it is rather expensive."

"For goodness sake girl just buy it if you like it, tell you what? I'll buy it for you!"

"But mum, you and dad will have to spend quite a lot for our holidays, so don't worry I'm going to pay for that myself, and no questions about it, you two spend enough money on me….."

"Nonsense girl, I will buy it for you..."

"Alright mum if you insist.. but let me tell you that I have quite a good and healthy account!"

"Don't kid yourself girl, money is hard to get and easy to go, dad and I had some experience about that, so look after your money okay?"

"I bet uncle John never had any problems about money!"

"No…He didn't because he married that rich woman, if you ask me he was a silly boy really!"

"Well mum if you are not happy in a relation, it's no use staying together!"

"True darling, but he…..your uncle took everything for granted, he started by neglecting his wife by looking at other skirts, and many skirts if I may say so!"

"I never thought he was as naughty as that mum!"

"Yes he was, I can't say this to your father, as I might upsetting him!"

"Yes, but if dad knows his brother done wrong, he should agree with you."

"True, but you know John is his only brother, and then he doesn't want to upset your granddad Tom and grandma Anne, I know how much they always glorified John."

"Did they? I didn't know that!"

"Yes they did and your father loves more his parents than his brother, that's why he decided to call you Suzanne when you were born, I know he done that to please his mother!"

"Of course mum, I knew that part of my name, is also related to grandma!"

"That's alright darling, and now let's do some more shopping, we need quite a few more things for our holiday.

"As I said mum many times I like uncle John very much, he's always been ever so kind, I think we almost have been like brother and sister!"

"In a way he's quite a good hearted soul, there was a time when he offered money to your dad, but he would never take any advantages, he likes to be very independent."

"Thank you for telling me all this mum, it's nice to know some stories from families."

"Well, I thought you should, as you are not any longer a little girl. I suppose you don't remember John's wife Gloria."

"Of course I do remember her mum, I must have been only eight then."

"Well she was not perfect, but she wasn't too bad, if anything he was the one to blame for their split up!"

"Well mum, I think I ought to make a confession."

"Come on girl don't keep me in suspense!"

"Few weeks ago I was washing this lady's hair, and as I was drying, she asked me if I knew who she was, I said no, and she said: "I am your uncle ex wife Gloria, I remember you when you were little, you were so pretty and you are prettier now, if you don't mind me saying so!"

"Nice to meet you Gloria, I'm sorry that you and my uncle are divorced."

"She said; "I'm sorry too Susanne, because I did love your uncle very much, and please don't mention me to your parents" In that moment Joanne took over for her perm, at the end she came to me, she gave me a tip and said: "Hope to see you again Susanne"

"That was very strange, because as far as I know she lives quite away from Greatstone."

"So you don't know where she lives mum."

"Not really, not even your dad knows, because they change house after their divorce...mind you we never talk about her or John's past.

"Shame really, it would be nice to talk about it sometimes, I see no arm,"

"Perhaps you are right Suzanne, I see no wrong in that, to be honest, her family is quite well off, if you know what I mean!"

"Actually she seemed to me quite pleasant too, in fact she didn't have to talk to me at all."

"True…I suppose not, but there again, how did she know that you were working in that place?"

"Yes, that is very odd indeed, and I think she saw me a few times before in incognito, that's what she said, and then finally came the time to reveal herself to me!"

"Why, I just can't make it out Suzanna, may I suggest that we should keep this episode to ourselves?"

"Yes mum, I think it's a good idea, I appreciate that."

"And I don't know whether your father would appreciate that, in any case I did, and I thank you for that."

"Thank you mum, I knew you would have appreciated it!"

"Good…and now let's get on with our spending spree."

"Ah, ah, ah, You are funny mum!"

Chapter 3

"Hello, where is everyone?

"We are in here dad, watching the six o/clock news."

"I thought you'd be busy doing the dinner darling!"

"It's all under control sweetheart, I've a nice roast in the oven, which won't be long!"

"Thank you darling, I'll go up stairs to have a wash, won't be long, tell you what I fancy a sherry when I come down, I've some good news for you two!"

"Then you can have a large one, provided that you don't fall asleep before dinner!"

"You are so funny Claire.!

"She's been like that all day long dad."

"You are not certainly getting a sherry, I'll tell you that!"

"Don't worry mum, I don't even like it, but I wouldn't mind a vodka and tonic."

"I beg your pardon, young lady, we don't keep vodka in our cup board."

"I'm only joking mum, mind you I shall have a couple of extra roast potatoes and an extra slice of beef, with lots of gravy!"

"That's my girl, you can have as much as you like!"

"Thank you for my pre-dinner drink, I'm not used to such luxury darling!"

"Take your glass with you everything it's on the table."

"This is really excellent Claire, so, did you buy all you wanted today?"

"Near enough dad, I think I nearly empty my bank account, but since we a few more weeks before our holidays, I shall recoup alright."

"Yes girls, we are going to close the garage for three weeks, and Jack was more than please, to take extra time off for himself too...for a change!"

"That's good of him Eddy, quite honestly I didn't think he would agree on that."

"Well...further more he's a bit fed up with his business, I mean he's not losing any money, apart from the fact he did say he has a lot of overheads....."

"What do you mean Eddy, does he want to sell up?"

"That's what he said, but if he decide to do so, I would get the first choice to buy him out..."

"Oh yes..... With what.... shirt buttons?

"Yes my dear....I thought the same as you, no way we could afford to buy his business...but..."

"But what? Come on then tell us, what else did he say?"

"Nothing else for the moment, he only told me, not to worry, that something can be worked out."

"Well, it sounds like he's making up his mind, how is he?"

"I think is approaching seventy, quite honestly I hope I'll be able to stop working earlier than that, just look at my father, he's clocking seventy and he looks eighty."

"Don't you start worrying about the age now darling, you look much younger than you are, if I may say so!"

"That's very kind to say that Claire!"

"I bet a lot of young birds are looking at you dad?"

"Don't be silly Suzanne..you mean old birds!"

"Don' say that mum, dad doesn't look as old as many others of his age, in fact some of mine working mates, mentioned that a few times, that I've got a young father, and a good looking father too."

"If you are after some money sweetheart, let me tell that you are unlucky."

"I knew you wouldn't believe me, honestly dad…"

"So…. your working mates told you that you have a young good looking father?"

"See what you done now Suzanne, you made your mother jealous… I find that very interesting, I didn't know that I could make women interested in me at my age!"

"Look at him, he sounds like Valentino, anyone for pudding?

"Yes thank you love, and then I shall make a phone call to John, hoping to find him available."

"Mind you when they say he's busy, he does always ring you back!"

"That's true Claire!"

"Hello….hello….Hotel Riviera speaking, can I help you?"

"Oh..Good evening, could I speak to John Collins please?"

"May I ask who's speaking?"

"Yes.. I am his brother speaking from England!"

"One moment please….. I'll try his office…."

"Hi Eddy, nice to hear from you, how are you, and everyone else?"

"We are fine thank you John, just to tell you that I can come a few days before the fifteen of July, but to be certain I'll have to get some dates from Jack, I think this year we are closing for three weeks, isn't that marvellous? As Jack wants to take a longer break too."

"That's wonderful Eddy, your hotel is semi book, just give me the date of arrival, tell you what, I would like you to arrive around lunch time so you and family can have lunch here at my hotel with me, and then I shall take you myself to the hotel where you'll be staying, it's only five minutes' walk.

"Thank you John, but we don't like to trouble you too much in your hotel, perhaps we can find it ourselves and book in"

"It's no trouble at all Eddy, the fact is that you cannot book in before three o/clock in the afternoon, so I thought if you get here for lunch we can have a bite to eat together and have a chat, after all I haven't seen you lot for a long time!"

"If you say so John, I will look forward to that, we shall come by car, we shall be arriving on the twelve of July, I'm sure of that, you can book the hotel for fourteen nights, make it one single and one double bedrooms!"

"Thank you Eddy, that's fine, one thing I must tell you, your hotel hasn't got a swimming pool, but you have a choice for the girls, you can use the beach which is very near or you can come to my hotel, we have three big swimming pools here!"

"Are you sure John? I hope this won't cause any problems, as we won't be staying there!"

"Eddy will you please stop worrying, just leave it to me, I only too please to do something for my family!"

"Thank you again John, is there anything else you'd like to know?"

"Nothing else Eddy, just give me a ring the day before you leave, I know you shall have to stop one night in France, may I suggest to make your stop somewhere near Lyon, so you'll be able to get here by lunchtime."

"I will do that John, and thank you for everything, you have been a great help, Claire and Suzanne say hello and they look forward to see you soon!"

"If there are any changes, please let me know Eddy, in the meantime lots of hugs to all of you, speak to you soon!"

"Thanks John….we'll do…bye, bye!"

"All done girls! He invited us at his hotel for lunch the day we arrive, because he wants to take us to our hotel himself."

"Oh..That's wonderful dad, I'm looking so forward to see my uncle, and for my holiday of course!"

"Darling we are all three of us looking forward for our holiday, do you realize that we haven't been away for five years, the last holiday we had it was at the camp site in Bittling, and that was terrible, the food was so bad that I still have the taste in my mouth!"

"You are right Claire, but things have improved since then, we are now living more or less like the continentals!"

"Yes Eddy, I think we should be part of Europe, but here we are glorifying with the spectacular fish and chips!"

"Nothing wrong with that mum, I love fish and chips!"

"Even that has improved now, before they used to eat it in newspaper…I ask you was that really fantastic?"

"Not really Claire, I must agree with you there!"

"There's a good film on the telly. Who's going to join me?"

"Go on you two, I'll clear up the table and I'll join you in ten minutes!"

"Many thanks mum, I think it was my turn tonight!"

"Go on.. join you daddy, and make sure he doesn't fall asleep, like last night!"

"The washing up is all done, What are you watching?"

"Mum I wanted so much to watch that love story we were talking about this morning, and what happened? Dad switched on to a cowboy film!"

"I suppose it's a John Waynny one, is that so Eddy?"

"Sorry Claire but I haven't seen this one, I read the review, and I think it's going to be a good one, actually I haven't seen a cowboy film for a long time, all they screen now are those terrible detective stories!"

"In a way you are right Eddy, to me they are all far-fetched, what do you think Suzanne?"

"You are right mum but I think I'll go and watch the telly upstairs, I'll join you Suzanne if you don't mind!"

"And you Mr. Collins don't make me come downstairs to wake you up......"

Chapter 4

(The day of their departure was very near in fact today was going to be the last working day for Eddy and Suzanne, Claire was already starting to get the suitcases ready and get the house all tide up, she thought to avoid any criticism from Eddy's parents, as they were the one to look after the house while they were away. So by the end of the evening almost everything was done, and now she was busy getting the dinner ready.)

"Hello darling, have been busy today, I see you still have the iron board standing in the washing room!"
"I say, of course I have been busy, I cleaned up the house from top to bottom!"
"Why did you have to do that for, we could have done on our return,. anyway, we still have tomorrow before we set off."
"Of course we have tomorrow, don't forget we don't have to do only the suitcases, there will be other things."
"Hello mum…Hi dad.. look what they gave me my at work. They all wish us a very happy holidays, and I think they all jealous because we are going to Italy"

"Let's have look Suzanne, that's very nice of them, lots, lotions, perfume, travelling staff, and two beautiful beach towels…so big they are…"

"I work with some lovely people mum, they are all really nice, and the boss, gave fifty pounds towards my holiday!"

"They are really good Suzanne, it means you are doing your job alright!"

"They said they will miss me, and so some of the customers!"

"that's good darling we are so proud of you!"

"Thanks mum, you are always so reassuring!"

"That's it darling, the car is all in order…"

"Are you sure Eddy, I know you are a good mechanic but make sure that you have checked everything!"

"Rest assure Claire that I started a month ago to make a list of what's to be done and prepare, for certain haven't missed anything!"

"Did you take the spare house keys to your parents."

"Yes darling and I told them not to over water the garden and flowers, in fact my father told me off for threaten him like a young kid!"

"I like that Eddy, I've got to say that parents never think that we grow up too!"

"You are so right Claire."

"Dinner will ready in ten minutes and then don't forget to ring your brother."

"All under control darling…. **(Looking at Suzanne while Claire goes into the kitchen)**

"Please dad don't say anything, I know the feeling!"

"Thank you Suzanne, I think that I must be a saint sometime…to support her nagging."

"Dad….She doesn't mean it, she's only trying to help, have you ever thought that in life we do forget things sometimes?"

"Perhaps you are right Suzanne, yes, I am forgetful sometimes!"

"See…I am right, because I tend to be forgetful too!"

"Dinner is ready…come and get it………"

"That was as usual first class Claire, thank you and those couple of glasses of wine just made it perfect!"

"So, now you can ring John darling."

"Just about to do it Claire…"

(John was very pleased to hear that they were ready to depart for their holiday, and of course Eddy was reminded to get to his hotel around lunch time the next day, as he was looking forward to get together after such a long time!")

(The next morning Suzanne woke up very early, and made a cup of tea for her parents, and in no time at all they were boarding the ferry. The crossing was very smooth as it was a beautiful day, Left Calais very early and between the two drivers, they managed to reach a small hotel near Turin, had a pleasant dinner and left early for the Italian Riviera, everything went beautifully thanks to the French and Italian beautiful motorways. They found the Hotel Riviera quite easily, as it was situated right on the sea front, and of course John was there to welcomed them and make them feel at ease. Just before lunch he took them around the vast hotel to show how beautiful it was.)

"Oh... uncle this is stupendous, you are a very lucky man, and I can see that you are very happy, and of course surrounded by people who think highly and respect you!"

"Maybe you are right Suzanne, but not hundred per cent, as in every job you always get that someone who jealous for what you are, and so you have to fight and be quite strict sometimes, and that is the only way you can maintain a little respect."

"I think you must be good at your job, I don't think dad wouldn't be able to a job like yours, he always said that, the continentals or the Irish people are good at it."

"He's probably right, actually I haven't met many English people working in catering business... anyway enough of this, you are here on holiday not to talk about work, and it's so nice to see you all and very happy, have you got a boyfriend yet?"

"Not really uncle, I haven't met anyone that I would like, lots of them, are a bit useless and very childish"

"What do you mean useless Suzanne?"

"Well, maybe I meant ambitious, like yourself uncle, I often thought that you always achieved what you wanted, I really do admire you for that!"

"You are too kind darling, I was more ambitious years ago, now unfortunately I'm getting older!"

"Older....? Am I right that you are only thirty this year?"

"Yes you are right darling.....I think we better call your mum and dad and go down to the swimming pool restaurant, there they have a good choice of cold meats and salads...Are you hungry...you better be because the choice is astronomical ?"

"Actually I am uncle, I love cold meat and salad, that's what I have when I have my lunch break from work"

"Help yourself folks, I'm going to find a nice table, would like some wine, beer soft drinks, just tell me and I will get them!"

"I think I shall have a nice beer John, how about you girls?"

"I think we shall have only soft drinks John thank you.."

"Thank you John, this is more than we expected, it's very kind of you!"

"Oh come off it brother, if I can't do this for my family, who do you think I should do it for, I really do consider you as my family, because I love you… How's mum and dad then Eddy?"

"They are alright, unfortunately they are getting old but they are fine, they send their love to you and they said they are missing you, I think you should visit them."

"Eddy I have been so busy in the past couple of years, then of course before that I went through that nasty divorce, which nearly bankrupt me, sort of saying, and some other things, I've been lucky really to have had jobs to keep me going, well…the rest is history!"

"I am not criticizing you John, in fact I admire you for your drive to make a few pounds, it's only mum and dad they worry me sometimes!"

"I understand Eddy, tell you what at the end of the summer I will come and visit them…and that's a promise!"

"You can stay with us uncle, mum is an excellent chef, she can cook some Italian dishes too!"

"Don't exaggerate Suzanne, I'm your English uncle and shall look forward to try some good old English pies!"

"You can say that again Claire, I would indeed, I think I'm getting fed up of pasta, and pasta again…ah, ah, ah, ah!"

"Actually Claire, I must say that your spaghetti are superb, I do rather enjoy them now and then!"

"So glad to hear that Eddy......Good afternoon Fred, hello Laura...hi Barry....Oh, let me introduce you to my family Fred..."

"Hi.... good afternoon John...of course."

"This is my brother Eddy, his wife Claire and daughter Suzanne and this is Fred...Fred Tender, his wife Laura and their son Barry!"

"Nice to meet you all, John did mentioned that you were coming for a couple of weeks. Are you staying in the hotel?"

"Not really, we are staying over the road!"

"Don't laugh Eddy, Fred come from Littlewood!"

"Is that so? We live in Greatstone, a stone throw from us, if you don't mind me saying so....ah, ah, ah, ah!"

"Yes, ah, ah, ah I do like a pun out of a coincidence!"

"Fred is a builder, actually once he was in partnership with my ex father in law!"

"Yes I was Eddy, but things didn't work out well, partnerships are like marriages, if you know what I mean, sorry about that John..."

"Don't worry about me Fred, you are not wrong there!"

"Well, in my opinion marriage is what you get out of it, and of course it's not an easy union, but sometime it has to be worked out on both sides!"

"That's very true Eddy, my Laura tends to nag me quite often, but I play the doffing part most of the times!"

"That's true, I keep telling to have his hearing checked!"

"They only listen what they want to hear Laura!"

"that's what I keep saying to my old man Laura!"

"Enough of the old man Claire, don't take any notice of my wife Laura!"

"Well said Eddy, come on then you two let's get some lunch…."

"See you later folks."

"See you later neighbours!"

"How about that for a coincidence Eddy?"

"That Barry seems a very quiet boy, he hasn't said a word uncle!"

"That's not what I think Suzanne, I think he's got his eyes on quite a few girls around this pool!"

"Is that so? He must be a silent lover then!"

"Suzanne…behave yourself…"

"Mum I'll be eighteen in a few days, stop treating me like a schoolgirl, where is the small room?"

"Over there on the left Suzanne……She quite a girl, if you don't mind me saying so Claire, what I mean she is young lady now, I don't blame her to tell you that!"

"Yes it's true John, maybe we should treat her like a young lady now, sometime I wish we another child!"

"Yes darling, maybe we should have had another one!"

"Oh there you are Suzanne, are you okay, now then don't forget you lot, if you wish to use the swimming pool instead of the beach you are welcome to come here, I shall give you a couple pass, to show at the entrance gates!"

"That's kind of you John, we do appreciate. What time are you taking us to that hotel?"

"In half an hour or so…. in the meantime enjoy your lunch, go and get some more if you like!"

Chapter 5

(John took his brother and family to the their hotel, namely Sea View Hotel, indeed stood by its name, overlooking that blue sea and its beautiful beaches.)

"Very nice place John, thank you for your choice, what's more the owner looks very hospitable, nice bedrooms with balconies, what else?, we seem to have everything we need.

"It's a demi-pension, which it mean breakfast and evening dinner, lunch there are so many little places, you'll have no problems."

Yes I understood that, anyway, I see that it's written in English, in the brochure too."

"So, if you need anything else please don't hesitate to call me, I think I'd better go back to the hotel now.

"Thanks for everything John, we are ever so grateful, see you later."

"Bye.. everyone…bye, bye Suzanne!"

"Bye uncle… see you soon, many thanks."

"Right then girls, let's unpack, then we can go for a walk down on beach."

(They went for walk and had leisurely drink on the beach and later they were back at the hotel for a nice shower.

Dinner was served at seven, and they thought it was very pleasant, followed a nice walk through the town, shops were all opened and restaurants and coffee bars were completely full with customers, the streets were well lit, everything really looked quite full of life...not really like Greatstone commented Suzanne, and as they were passing by a beautiful coffee bar place they noticed Fred Tender's and family having a few drinks.)

"Hello Eddy, nice to see you again and hello all."

"Oh hello Fred, I see you are enjoying an after dinner drink."

"Indeed dear Eddy, why don't you join us, go on we only need one more chair, Barry pull that chair up here."

"Many thanks Fred, I hope we are not intruding......"

"Nonsense Eddy, come on Claire and.....Suzanne is it? I almost forgot your name!"

"No... you've got it right Mr. Tender...!"

"Ah, ah, ah, Mr. Tender I like that, for goodness sake just call me Fred, not even my own staff are allowed to address me as Mr. Tender, what would you like to drink?

"Thanks Fred a beer for me a couple of soft drinks for the girls...."

"Thank you for ordering for us Eddy (**Claire replied)**

"Sorry darling I know you only drink soft drinks!"

"Dad is right mum...many thanks Fred...."

"That's what I like girls....a bit of understanding between the two of you"

(While they were all having their drinks Suzanne and Barry sat on the side and started to get acquainted.)

"So…. nice to meet you Suzanne, funny I never had the chance to see you in Greatstone, as I nearly come every day, I have quite a few friends there."

"Oh yes? I work in Lawrence Hairdresser five days a week, so, I am really in town almost every day!"

"I was wondering……I know you are not staying in our hotel, why don't you try the swimming pool there, I might ask the guard at the gates to let you in!"

"No need for that Barry, I have a special pass from my uncle, and I can come whenever I like.!

"That's wonderful then, tomorrow, come over and we can have a swimming competition…You can swim, can you?"

"Of course I can, I won a couple first prices in my school days,"

"Good, you know I find it quite boring in this hotel, I can hardly find someone who to talk to!"

"As a matter of fact, I saw quite a few youngsters around that pool today, it seems to me very odd that you say that!"

"Yes there are, but quite a few of them almost all Italians, are so stuck up, I don't know what it is, could it be the language barrier?"

"I don't really know, as I am not acquainted with the Italian mentality."

"They seem to be so different than us, but they very good hearted, and polite."

"I presume they are, as you can see my uncle is very happy to work amongst them…And believe me, he wouldn't stay here if he didn't like them."

"Hello you chatter box, time to go and let these nice people, enjoy their evening, furthermore we are tired after all that travelling."

"Here we go Barry, I hope your parents don't dictate like mine do…"

"I better no comment to that Suzanne…ah, ah, ah, "

"I heard that young lady!"

"Don't worry Suzanne, they are probably right to say they are tired, but please, will you come at the hotel swimming pool tomorrow?"

"Of course I will Barry, see you tomorrow at ten in the morning…Bye, bye for now and thanks for the drinks!"

"Thanks for the company Fred, might see you tomorrow!"

"Good night Claire…night Eddy…."

"Nice people don't you think so Eddy? Quite honestly I think you should have offered to pay for the drinks."

"Don't worry Claire next time I will pay for the drinks, after all it was only a small beer and a couple of soft drinks."

"No matter what kind of drinks, but I think it's nice to return their kindness."

"Alright…alright…I said I will pay them back, didn't I?"

"Stop arguing you two, after all I think mum is right, you don't want to show yourself meaner than anybody else!"

"Sorry Claire, I suppose you are right, next time I'll insist to pay for the drinks, I promise!"

"That's what I like to hear, let us be a bit more smarter!"

(First breakfast at the Hotel Sea View and they seem to be in their holiday gear for the great sunshine.)

"I slept like a log Claire, and this breakfast is really good, I mean it's not eggs and bacon and baked beans, but at least they have boiled eggs and so many other things!"

"Yes dad it's quite nice, there's more here than we could wish for!"

"I heard you talking to Barry last night. Are you going to the hotel swimming pool then Suzanne?"

"Yes, I think I will, after all I promised I would!"

"Okay then, me and dad are going down on the beach and we'll be right opposite our hotel, if you come and look for us you know we are there, if not we know where you are we shall come and get you away from Barry!"

"No need for mum, I know how to control him, don't worry, I could read his little mind!"

"Okay then girl, behave yourself, if there are any problems, your uncle is at hand….here take this pass it will help you to get in!"

"Thanks mum… see you later…bye dad!"

"There you are Suzanne, I really thought that you wouldn't come, I've got those two chairs in that corner where you get some shade, is that alright?"

"I don't mind the sun Barry, that's what I'm here for, I want to go back to England nice tanned!"

"So do I Suzanne, shall we have a good swim?"

"Off you ho then Barry, I challenge you to that end!"

(So the competition started)

"Sorry Barry, I didn't mean to show off, I can see your parents are laughing!"

"They would, they like to see me trashed to pieces!"

"Don't say that Barry, I tell what, I'll go off first and I will let you win, how's that for fairness?"

"Okay…off you go then….. and take it easy okay?
"Don't worry Barry…."

(And Barry got there first, his parents were not laughing but clapping)

"Thank you Suzanne, I owe you a drink, come on it's my turn to make you happy!"
"Thank you for the drink Barry, isn't nice just to sit here in the sun with a lovely drink?"
"You just can't beat that especially if I am sitting next to a beautiful girl…(**Holding her hand**)
"Barry I think you rushing things now, your parents are looking at us and perhaps wondering what's going to happen."
"So sorry Suzanne, I didn't meant, I just done it spontaneously, please forgive me!"
"Of course you are forgiven, actually it wasn't a nasty touch, you've got quite warm hands!"
"Gosh….now you make me blush, but I think I will overcome the excitement!"
"Oh good morning you two, glad you found some company of your age Suzanne. I guess mum and dad are down on the beach"
"Hello uncle, how are you today? Yes Barry and I had a swimming race, he traced me the second time….And yes mum and dad are there somewhere holding hands!"
"Ah, ah, ah, I like that sweetheart, I don't think my brother is doing that, maybe years ago **(John's phone rung)** Ah, this phone never stop ringing…sorry guys….""Hello.. Oh yes? tell him to sit in the reception, I'll be there in a minute, thanks! Sorry guys somebody wants my attention, see you later…enjoy!"

"Must say your uncle speaks good Italian!"
"Well…I think he's in this country for more than five years, then of course he speaks other languages!"
"That's interesting Suzanne, it must nice to be able to connect with foreigners!"

(In the meantime John arrived in the reception)
"Oh hello Roberto, I thought I sent you a message!"
"Sorry John but we did not receive any message at all, and the boss is doing his nut, he wants his money!"
"Look just tell him that as soon as I get hold of some he'll be the first to be paid off, he should know by now that I never let him down over the years!"
"Look John I know you mean well, and I really like you, but let me tell you something, I know our boss in and out, and I rather not upset him as he can do something drastic."
"For goodness sake, I might give him a ring today, and tell him myself!"
"I wouldn't do that if I were you, he doesn't want no calls accept from his family, as he's always suspicious that his calls are being intercepted!"
"Alright then Roberto, try to persuade him, you owe me this favour!"
"Okay John, I will, I hope I'll make him understand!"
"Many thanks Roberto, I really do appreciate that!"
"Tell you what John after, if you don't mind I shall give you a ring later on, and tell you his reaction."
"Okay Roberto, but be careful what you say on the phone, you never know who's listening!"
"I know that John, don't worry…speak to you later. Bye."
"Bye, bye Roberto and thank you!"

Chapter 6

(As soon as Roberto left, John thought to make a phone call to his ex wife)

"Hello… Hello who's that? Oh..is you John, how are you?"
"I'm well thank Doreen , look I'm ringing from Italy, could I speak to Gloria please? It's quite important!"
"I think she's upstairs, hold on I call her…..Gloria it's for you…From Italy!"
"Hello John, what's happening then? I gather that you ringing me because you are in trouble!
"Come on Gloria, there's no need to be like that, look I've been a bit unlucky lately, I'm going to honest with you I had a car accident and of course I didn't know that my insurance had expired by a couple of days, and as I parked the car I badly damaged the car in front of me, you can imagine the owner when he found out that I had no insurance, although I said I would pay for the damages, which were about one thousand pounds or less, this chap wanted two thousand pounds if I didn't agree he would go to the police, now in a situation like that, I would be locked up for certain and lose my European license , so I am desperate for a couple of thousand pounds as soon as possible, and get rid of that bastard!"

"John this is not the first time I bail you out, I know you were quite generous when we parted and left me the half of the house, only because you went abroad, and that was your choice!"

"Come off it Gloria, I promise I will pay you back, I know I made a few mistake when we were married, but you can't say that I was mean to you, and I must admit darling I still love you, in fact I wish you would come and visit me, I've got a top job now!"

"Well John I've got an idea, I will accept your offer, it will be nice to meet your brother, Claire and Suzanne, I know they are staying with you!"

"Good lord…news travel fast, how did you know about my brother and family?"

"Quite simple really I use the hairdresser where your darling Suzanne works, she's a lovely girl really, last time I introduce myself, she was quite surprised as she didn't recognized me, that girl she thinks the world of you!"

"Yes she does really, I think my brother is lucky to have a nice wife and a lovely daughter, pity we didn't have any kids, although they tried very hard!"

"Did they? Pity we didn't have any... I'm quite happy we didn't, with our divorce they would be suffering now!"

"Maybe if we had even one, we wouldn't have had to divorce!"

"Is your brother and family staying with you?"

"Well actually they are not, but they are staying next door to us a beautiful three stars hotel, much cheaper that the one I work for, and yes why don't you come down, you would be most welcome, I've got room in my little chalet."

"I think I will, I will try and book the flight for tomorrow, so I can take that money with me, and you can pay me back for a nice bedroom in your hotel!"

"That's okay then Gloria, just let me know the time of your arrival and I shall come to pick you up at the airport!"

"I will ring you in a couple of hours…okay John?"

"Fantastic Gloria, I'm really looking forward to see you and don't forget that little envelope!"

"Speak to you soon John…."

"Bye, bye Gloria…love you!

(Meanwhile Suzanne and Barry down at the swimming pool are still enjoying their swimming)

"Barry…. dad and I are going to have a bite to eat, would you like to come?"

"Okay mum I'll join you in a minute…Would you like something to eat Suzanne?"

"Not really, I had a big breakfast this morning, you go and join your parents!"

"Can I bring you back something? I don't have to pay, you know?"

"Neither do I, I can use my pass if I want something!"

"Okay then Suzanne, I'll only be half an hour!"

"Hello Suzanne, where is Barry then has he already divorced you?"

"You can shout uncle, can't understand why you split up with Gloria, did you know that I met her?"

"Well….yes and no but I've got news for you, for mum and dad, she's coming down to visit me, maybe tomorrow or the next day, and she'll be staying in this hotel!"

"That'll be nice uncle, and it will give me a chance to meet her properly, and find out about your crafty escapades!"

"Sweetheart, don't you believe what you hear, sometimes people are very good on discrediting their own friends!"

"I didn't mean that uncle, I think you are a nice guy, and what I like about you is that you always have a smile for everyone, and that says something about a person, or shall I say a smile on your face it's like a ray of sunshine!"

"Good lord, thank you, thank you! You are a poetess too now, come here darling I want to embrace you…**(And so uncle John gives Suzanne a nice friendly cuddle and a gentle kiss on her forehead)** you're a darling!" **(An elderly lady sitting by watched and smiling, which made John saying**: "She's my adorable niece…you know?" **(The lady replied;)** "You are a very lucky uncle, my husband and I never had that fortune!"

(Suzanne was somehow speechless for a few seconds, looking in his uncle' eyes she felt a sensational feeling, maybe that was her first body language sensing an attraction perhaps with each other)

"Yes uncle, even mum has said many times that you are not all that bad, unlike your parents always say that you are a gigolo, you know I had to look on the dictionary for the meaning of that word!"

"I am not really….that word has many meanings, I would say the main one it would be a playboy, but nothing much really, don't take any notice of your grand's, no matter what they say I love them both to bits!"

"I loved them too uncle, I hope they look after my two little budgies."

"I'm sure they will, you know they love you too…hello young man Barry…"

"I've got a little panino sandwich and a soft drink Susanne, you just cannot go without eating something!"

"Oh thanks Barry, that's very kind of you."

"See you later you two and enjoy your swimming!"

"See you later uncle and thank you!"

"Don't mention it darling….love you!"

"He really like you Suzanne…"

"And I like him, he's my only uncle, and he's always been nice to my mum and dad!"

"I see what you mean Suzanne, I have three uncles and to be honest they don't even know I exist!"

"Do you visit them sometimes?"

"Not really… my father he's too busy making money, and my mother is too busy with her friends, money can play sadness as much as happiness sometimes!"

"True Barry…very true indeed, I know some families not as well off as some but they are very happy, I think I shall go and find my parents now, they probably wonder what has happened to me."

"Can I see you tomorrow Suzanne?" **(touching her hand again)**

"Of course Barry, **(Smiling)** I think tomorrow I try to bring my parents too!"

"Why not Suzanne..and maybe one afternoon we can go down on the beach and hire one of them pedal-boat, that will be fun.."

"We'll see Barry, anyway, thank you for your company today, I really did enjoy very much, and of course we might see you later on for a drink in that coffee bar."

That'll be nice Suzanne, I shall look forward to that, I'll see you later then."

"Yes…bye..bye..say hello to your parents when they come back!"

"I will Suzanne...Thank you!"

(Meanwhile John gets a phone call from Roberto regarding his boss decision, but John has a new idea of how to pay back his debt.)

"Oh hello it's you Roberto, so what's happening then?"
"That's okay John he said he can give you a week as from yesterday, and I will picking it up at the hotel!"
"Now listen Roberto, as you know I am struggling to get this money, so I came up with a new idea, which you could pass on to your boss!"
"Fire away my friend…"
"Well, instead of giving you the cash, I could offer your boss two weeks fully paid here at this hotel whenever he likes, and that the cost to stay here, would be double the amount I owe him, can you pass it on?"
"Since you are my friend John, I will tell him, I will ring you back later on!"
"Many thanks Roberto, you are a chum!"

(Meanwhile Suzanne join her parents on the beach)
"Hello mum hello dad, I see you've got a very nice spot, secluded from that nasty little wind!"
"Actually that keep us cool, because it's so hot today, I wish we this weather in England!"
"I've got a bit of news for you dad…. guess what….?"
"I have no idea darling, don't tell me that my parents are coming down here too!"
"Ah, ah, ah, nothing like that but something similar, uncle John just told me that his ex wife is coming down in the next day or so!"
"You are joking of course Suzanne."
"No… it's true and she's staying in the hotel,"
"Surely he's not paying for it, the rascal is always penniless."
"What do you mean dad, I'm sure with the job he's got, living in with food an all…he should save quite a lot!"

"One thing you don't know about your uncle, first he's very generous, second he spend his money like we use water in the morning, yes in the past he had some good jobs, but somehow in can't save up for his rainy days!"

"Right darling let's go back to the hotel, we'll have a nice shower then we can have a couple of glasses of wine, we bought two bottles yesterday, we'll have a couple of glasses and we can take the rest down in the restaurant!"

"Jolly good idea Eddy, let's do that!"

"Mum are you sure that you can take your own wine in the restaurant?"

"I don't see why not everyone drunk wine last night during dinner!"

"Yes, I think I noticed that they ordered their wine, maybe I'm mistaken I think we ought to ask at the reception, you don't want to take a bottle and be told that you can't drink it!"

(When arrived at the hotel Claire approached the girl behind the reception)

"Good evening madam, we have some wine which a friend gave us can we take down and drink during our dinner?"

"No madam, you cannot do that, if you are taking your wine you'll be charge corkage!"

"What do you mean corkage, I don't understand!"

"It means that we have to charge you five euro a bottle for your own wine, I think you better buy our, which will cost you only four euro, but you may drink it in your bedroom and there you will not be charged, but don't forget that the drinks and beers in the little fridge in your bedroom are not free, the chambermaid checks them every morning!"

"We knew that......As for the wine, That's very fair we thought perhaps we could have brought ours as it was a present, but in that case we will buy a bottle in the restaurant."

"Madam if you like I will ask my boss if he let you bring your own for nothing."

"No please don't do that, we shall buy our own, thank you!"

"We are always here to help you and please you madam, please do not be shy!"

"That's very kind of you....what's your name, as we are staying for two weeks!"

"My name is Angela, I'll be here every days!"

"My compliments Angela you speak very good English!"

"Thank you! I work in London for two years madam!"

"Nice to talk to you and thank you very much for your help, you were very helpful indeed!"

"Thank you madam, have a very nice evening!"

"Well that is sorted out alright, thank you Suzanne, you were right about the wine good job we asked, otherwise we would looked right Charlie the three of us, only in England you can take your wine!"

"Yes darling.....You know why?"

""No I don't, as well know I am not a wine drinker!"

"You don't have to be a wine drinker to know certain things, the problem that you can take wine in certain restaurants in England is because the wine is so expensive in the restaurant, these restaurateurs they ripping off the customers left right and centre."

"Yes Eddy, once again you are absolutely right!"

"After dinner can we go in that coffee bar for a drink tonight dad?"

"I don't see why not my darling, and tomorrow what date is it, I seem to have forgotten!"

"You are very funny Mr. Collins, come on the let's get ready for dinner...... and don't order the most expensive wine too!"

"I'll order what I want, some celebrations start early!"

(Roberto rings back with his answer)

"Hello Roberto, goodness me that was quick!"

"Yes, luckily I found him just in time, I told him about your idea, unfortunaly he said that he prefer his yacht, when it comes to have a holiday, I think he like his privacy."

"Shame really it would have been a good bargain for him, two weeks here for two people cost about four thousand euro!"

"However, he also suggested, as he hasn't paid me for two months, would it be alright for you if my wife and I come to your hotel for a couple of weeks? That would square up your debt, and also it would suit my boss, as he just about to leave for a few week on his yacht."

"Yes that would be okay, first of all I would like that in black and white, not that I don't trust you, but just to make sure your staying here will square up my problem!"

"You just do a letter John, and I will sign it, so you'll have no problem with Mr. Boss."

"I wish I knew your name of your boss, this boss business doesn't convince me a great deal, never thought about this before as I dealt with you, just the same..."

"Come on John, what different does it make his name or mine?"

"Okay I will do a letter, some kind of agreement, but you must let me know the date you will come with your lady, so I know exactly what to put on."

"that's no problem John, I think if you put on the date from next Monday, that would suit me fine, I think the big boss will leave tomorrow!"

"Do you know when he'll be back?"

"Not really, he only disclose certain details only to his brother!"

"His brother's not going with him then, not really, his brother is got his own yacht too!"

"Bloody hell…. they seem to doing alright, no wonder they charge a fortune for that staff, and you and here we are flogging it for peanuts."

"You are right my good friend, we are doing the dirty job, and most likely we can get caught before them."

"Let me clear about our agreement, I will say on the letter that I bought some kind of jewelry at the price of two thousand euro, that will be my security, then you'll make out that you are a relative of mine!"

"That will suits me fine, when will I sign that agreement?"

"The day you will book in the hotel, I'll see you next Monday then..what is your surname Roberto…."

"Roberto Ruta…."

"Don't forget that you'll need some ID when you book in, I'll see you on Monday three pm Roberto!"

"See on Monday John, you won't regret this, I shall look forward to enjoy my free holiday, I mean paid by my Boss!"

Chapter 7

"That was really a good wine which we had in the restaurant, I can't believe it was only four euro fifty, that was roughly four pound, in England you'd have paid fifteen pounds…not bad I'd say!"

"Yes dad, people I work with in the shop, go out a lot to restaurants, and they keep saying how expensive the drinks are."

"Goodness me Eddy, I've never seen so many holiday makers, not even as many went we went to Cornwall."

"Claire you can't compare Cornwall to the Italian Riviera, I bet you any money you like you won't see millionaires walking around Newtown."

"I must agree with you there Eddy…Oh here we are let's sit over there I just fancy a nice cappuccino."

"I'll have one too mum…"

"And I think I shall have one of their superb beer… and a large one!"

"Really when you look at those people, it make you think that is another way of life!"

"This is really beautiful Claire, I think we have been missing out a lot in life, from now on we shall take our yearly holiday abroad, if you don't mind."

"You could have two holidays a year you two, now that I am eighteen, you don't have to take me with you, you go and enjoy yourself."

"She's got a good point there Eddy, we have no other problems, we are not reach but we can enjoy ourselves moderately.!

"That's my big girl now....sorry I didn't mean big as fat, big as grown up...ah, ah, ah, ah."

"I know what you meant dad..."

"This beer is superb.... Hello Fred fancy seeing you here for the second day running...come on then, please join us for a drink!"

"Hello Laura, did have a nice day?"

"Very nice, but too quiet for my liking."

"Never mind take it easy while you are on holiday, I guess you'll be quite busy when you go back to England!"

"Busy? You must be joking Claire, you mean gallivanting with her ladies friends!"

"So what? If I could help you to lay bricks I would certainly do something different that sitting in the office, let me correct you... not gallivanting!"

"Sorry dear...I'd be lost without your brains!"

"Yes you would be, am I not right Barry?"

"Yes you are...can we have a drink now please?"

"Yes of course...I didn't dear asking you before your family meeting!"

"I'll have a nice beer like you Eddy....thanks."

"I'll have a crème de menthe frappe."

"And a small beer for me please....."

"Wonderful.....waiter...waiter....."

"I've got to be honest with you Laura, I've never see a crème de menthe in England

"I don't think you can get in an ordinary pub, unless you go to some of them high class places in London!"

"I must say though, in certain things Italians are more advanced than us!"

"Well, they are where ever you go in the continent!"

(They spent a couple hours discussing various facts of life, and their continental customs, obviously Suzanne and Barry were getting a bit bored, but they seem to put up, after all, the evening was for the parents to leisurely relax.)

(Suzanne woke up very early next morning, perhaps she thought of her birthday and so she was already was downstairs in the restaurant waiting for mum and dad.)

"Good morning sleepers, what's this then? the day started long ago…."

"Alright birthday girl just because is your big day and you want to make it longer, there's no need to be smarter, here you'll find all your goodies in this big sac!"

"Oh thanks mum, many thanks dad, I love you so much!"

"Happy birthday Suzanne, and these are all the cards from almost the people you know and families!"

"Oh.. I must ring grandma and granddad later, to thank them for everything, I finished my breakfast, while you're having yours I will open all the cards, I shall open the presents up in my room!"

"You do as you like girl, it's your big day today…!"

"I think I'll wait to open the presents, when you finish your breakfast mum, as you were getting your breakfast, the waitress seeing all these cards, she wished me happy birthday, she said it in Italian too."

"What a lovely gesture, I'm sure you said thank you!"

"Of course I did mum."

(After their breakfast they went upstairs, spread the cards around the bedroom, and look at the present, after which they went for a long walk on the beach. Lunch time was approaching and they thought to have a light lunch in one the small bistro on the beach)

"This is just what I wanted for lunch dad, cold chicken and salad, I see you are getting used to your pasta dad and how is your lasagne mum?"

"I couldn't have done them better, they are really soft and well seasoned!"

"Dad do you mind if I go back to the hotel this afternoon, I promised Barry that I would see him later."

"No need to ask girl, you do as you please, didn't we say that is your big day today?"

"Thank you, but I like you to know where I am, just in case you want me."

"Thank you dear for your concern, when you finish we shall walk back with you and you can stop at the swimming pool and we will have a nice walk around d the town, as we haven't seen much of it during the day."

"That's lovely dad, I'll probably be back at our hotel around five thirty!"

"do you have to get your swimming gear Suzanne?"

"Not really…. I already have it on as I thought I would pop there."

"I see you are organized darling…just like your father!"
"Well.. you've got to be organized in this world otherwise you will never achieve your goal!"

(They walked back and soon after they split up)
"See you later… don't spend too much dad!"
"I knew you were going to say something like that!"

"Hello Barry.. I bet you thought I wasn't going to come."
"Yes I did Suzanne…Happy birthday darling, hope you don't mind me calling you darling, you look so beautiful today!"
"Of course I don't mind, no arms in it, and thank you for your nice compliment, you make me blush."
"Well, I can't say any different from that, as you are really astonishing in them shorts!"
"I don't see your parents today, have they gone for an excursion?"
"Not really, I think they went for a walk, actually they said that wanted to see how the local market was, they quite a few leaflets in the reception, by the look of it, it seems to be quite big."
"Well, I think you see one market and see them all!"
"Shall we have a swim Suzanne!"
"Come on then Barry, I challenge you… no cheating!"

(They enjoyed their swimming for about half an hour and then they slouch in their chairs exhausted.!)

"Hello Barry, are you sleeping, I thought I heard a noise!"
"I don't think it me Suzanne, I think you must have fell asleep for ten minutes, I nearly called you, as I wouldn't like to see you burnt by the sun!"

"Yes I think I am getting a bit red, if you don't mind I must go to the ladies!"

"I think they are both out of order Suzanne, I suggest you use the one in the reception area!"

"Thanks for telling me Barry…I will… I'm glad I brought with me this veil, I wouldn't dear to walk in there in my swim costume!"

"You are right, it's forbidden to walk around the hotel semi-necked."

"See you in a few minutes Barry!"

"Shall I get you a coffee or an ice-cream?"

"A white coffee will do thanks Barry!"

(Found the ladies alright, as she was coming out uncle John was walking across)

"Hello sweetheart, and a very happy birthday to you, **(and looking toward the receptionists)** She's eighteen today, you know? And this is my beautiful niece…."

"Happy birthday young lady….**(They all shouted)**

"Thank you…thank you, are so kind of you all!"

"Come on darling, I've got something for you in my office, I couldn't let you become older without giving a present!"
(They both went in his office, went to his desk and took a little parcel from one of his draws)

"Gosh uncle this a beautiful office, not even the prime minister of England has one like it!"

"Never mind the beauty of this office, what most important is the beauty of my darling Suzanne, this is for you sweetheart,**(Giving the little parcel)**I hope you like it, it might make your mum jealous or it might make your dad envious as he loves you so much!"

"Oh thank you uncle, I don't know what to say, thank you so much...**(they hug simultaneously, John tries to kiss her on her forehead but Suzanne kisses him passionately on his lips and they embrace each other with fondness like two people in love...speechless they look at each other for a few seconds and then.....)**

"I'm so sorry Suzanne, I didn't want this to happen, please forgive me...."

"It wasn't your fault uncle, it's me, for some reasons I can't stop thinking of you...I should say sorry!"

"But darling do you realize what something like this will cause, not so much to me, but to your parents, and I would be disgraced forever!"

"But uncle, please help me to put out this obsession I have for you......It's something I just cannot control."

"I just don't know what to say anymore, and be aware that tomorrow Gloria will be here and for goodness sake let's play it cool!"

"Come on uncle you are making a drama out of a little kiss, yes I must admit just your touch gave me shivers right down my spine, that was lovely."

"Goodness me girl, I've had a few women in my life but no one ever knew how to talk like you!"

"Please uncle, don't reject me, I want your friendship very near me, that's the only way one day I might tell you, this is the end."

"Please try to think that I am your uncle and nothing else!"

"Oh I wish I could find someone like you to fall in love, instead there I meet an insipid fellow like Barry, that's all he wants to do.. is swimming, and maybe make out that he fancy women, I'm not so sure about that, as I see so many fellows now days on the other side of the fence!"

"You mean homosexuals liking each other?"

"That's alright uncle that the simple truth!"

"There again what can be done to change this…?"

"Nothing I'm afraid…the world's gone crazy, I think I better join Barry, I wonder what he might think!"

"I think you better my darling, and try to be nice to him, he might be a good future husband!"

"Do you really think so uncle….?"

"No.....I'm quite sure about that!"

"Maybe you are right, I will try my best.....!"

"You better darling.... See you later.....!"

"Be Good... uncle.....ah, ah, ah, ah!"

Chapter 8

"Hello Suzanne, you are late, I started to worry about you, I thought maybe something had happened!"

"Thank you for your concern Barry, but everything's alright, just that I met my uncle, he wished me happy birthday by giving me a present and so we started talking about family matters and so on…"

"Thant's okay Suzanne, my parents came around and wanted to wish happy birthday too, but you were delayed, they went up to their room, my mum said she had a terrible headache."

"So what did he give you your uncle, anything nice?"

"It's in this box, I think he gave me some perfume."

"You mean you have not opened it yet!"

"No…I thought I open it later on!"

"I find that a bit unusual Suzanne, usually presents should be open at receiving time, especially girls are so happy to get them!"

"True, in any case I said thank you to my uncle, and tomorrow I might thank him again…. did you know that his ex wife is joining him tomorrow?"

"Yes I heard my parents talking about it, I think they know her, she doesn't live very far from our house!"

"You probably know her yourself when you see her!"

"I might do, but I don't remember what she look like, my father say she's very attractive, and a very intelligent woman...Pity she's divorce from your uncle!"

"I met her when I was little, then I met her where I work, I was washing her hair, and she introduced herself to me, that was quite a surprise."

"Did you tell your parents about it."

"Yes, but I think they don't like to interfere in other people matters, especially now they are divorced!"

"Still, it's nice to see that they are still friendly…"

"That might be true but if I was married to someone, and then divorced, I certainly wouldn't like to be friendly, with my ex husband, I think true love it hard to get, but once it's achieved should last forever!"

"Your opinion is good, but not all partnerships are perfect, I mean husband and wife."

"Yes Barry… and the reason why is because honesty is hard to come by."

"I like your conversation, I find it very interesting, for a girl of your age I congratulate you."

"Thank you Barry…I am eighteen and how old are you?"

"Twenty Suzanne…twenty one very soon!"

"I thought you were younger than that, however, I think I better make a move, it's nearly five thirty, I promised my parents not to be late…. can I see you tomorrow Barry?"

"What a silly question Suzanne, of course darling, and I shall look forward, I find your conversation very interesting, not many girls now days can talk like you do. Bye for now…."

"Bye, bye Barry, be good…."

(Unfortunately this time there was no touching hands between the two, Barry felt a bit disappointed!"

"Come you two, I have been ready for the ten minutes!"
"Eddy why don't you go down in the restaurant and wait for us there…. I'm doing Suzanne's hair…….Oh, don't forget to order a bottle of bubbly, maybe Asti, that's a bit sweeter than the prosecco…."
"No problems Claire, don't be too late, I'm starving!"

"There you are you slow coaches, I was so thirsty that I thought of drinking a little beer, hope you don't mind!"
"Not at all dad, if I knew that I could have bought it for you."
"I didn't pay for it, I just put on the grand bill, tell you what darling, you can pay the whole bill at the of the holiday!"
"Thank you for taking me on holiday for my eighteen birthday and presenting me the bill, that's typical of you men!"
"Would I really?"
"I wouldn't put it past you…young man!"
"Changing subject I have decided…I'm going to have a little risotto start and then I'd like to try Veal in mushroom sauce, I haven't had veal since they stop selling it in England!"
"I think I'll join you Eddy…"
"Me too mum….."
"Right let me catch the waiter's eye…"

"As usual everything was perfect, I must tell my brother for his this hotel good choice, I think we'll have to chose the sweet now, look at the choice tonight!"

"Hello, hello.. now the lights have gone out....what's that?"

(A waitress was coming towards their table with a beautiful birthday cake, singing happy birthday......Yes it was for Suzanne eighteen.)

"You didn't tell me that you organized that Eddy!"

"Me? I did not I promise you....Claire."

"Look who's coming in dad...."

"Good lord is Fred, Laura and Barry!"

"So sorry to intrude, we thought we invite ourselves, for this beautiful event, and if you don't mind I just ordered a bottle of nice Prosecco to go with the cake!"

"So, I expect it was your idea Laura!"

"Indeed it was. I just couldn't let go your beautiful Suzanne without a special cake, and when I saw it today, I thought that is exactly fit for that beautiful girl, and my Barry smiled and said; why not mum, she deserve it....I hope you didn't mind Claire!"

"We are overwhelmed, just don't know what to say!"

"Thank you so much… I think I going to cry…Oh, you are so kind, thank you all of you, you just completed my grand day in style!"

(After finishing their cake and Prosecco, they all went for a nice walk and ended in their usual coffee bar for a night cup and long chat)

(The next day in the afternoon John was welcoming his friend Roberto and what he thought his wife, a good looking blond in her thirty, with a lot of make up on, and quite common by the way she walk and talk, He took them both to the reception to sign the register and to show their ID, after this John made Roberto sign their agreement, which that made John quite satisfied.)

"Nice to meet you Signora Tura, I hope you will have a very pleasant holiday!"

"Thank Signor John, and nice to meet you too."

"There you are Roberto, these are the keys, your room is on the fifth floor number 555, I see you only have a small suitcase, is that enough for the two weeks?"

"That's no problem John, we live just outside the town, if we need anything we can just pop over to our house and get what we need."

"I see what you mean Roberto, that's very handy, I suppose it's nice to travelling light!"

"Yes it is John….Come on Rita, let's go and change, then we can have a dip in the swimming pool."

"I'm coming Roberto….oops these high heels annoy me, I hope you my flat shoes in the suitcase!"

"I don't remember darling, you can always buy a pair of flip flops in that shop!"

"That's a good idea, come on then let's go up stairs!"

(John was a bit perplexed, if anything very curious, they didn't look like husband and wife, but there again, I can be wrong, he thought at least I'll be free of that problem, once for all, and I shall keep the two thousand pounds from Gloria to myself)

"Signor Collins, there's a phone call for you!"

"Thank you Jean, I will take in my office, on the private line, I expect it will be from my ex wife!"

"Hello…who am I speaking to?"

"Oh hello…My name is Roberto Tura, am I speaking to John Collins?"

"Indeed you are sir…"

"Last week you had a visit from a confident of mine regarding your Fifteen hundred euro that you own me, unfortunately I haven't seen him since."

"Excuse me, did you say that your name is Roberto Tura? Yes, someone came to see me about that money, and his name was Roberto Tura, are we having a mixed up names by any chance?"

"No... John I am Roberto Tura, can you describe the Roberto Tura that came to see you last week!"

"Well...a medium size chap with moustaches, wearing dark glasses, jeans and blue shirt!"

"I know, his name is Giorgio Zucchi and he's been doing a few jobs for me, he was suppose to collect that money from you, but I haven't seen him since!"

My dear Signor Tura, he did collect the money from me, and he told me that it was two thousand instead of fifteen hundred, as I was late paying it. So I gave him two thousand euro in cash and I made him sign a piece of paper, and his signature is Roberto Tura, I asked him if he could tell me who he's was working for, he told me; we all call him boss, and he added; that's what he wants to be called, and he told me that you spend a lot of time on your yacht!"

"The bastard thief, you just wait I get my hands on him, I'll trash him to pieces, and let me tell you that I haven't got a yacht!"

"I'm sorry for you Signor Tura that you have untrustworthy people working for you. However, if you want to see the piece of paper he signed, you can always come and see me, or if you want a copy I will posted to you!"

"If I'll require a copy I will let you know, in the meantime I thank you for your help!"

"Before you go Signor Tura, may I make it clear that I do not wish to have any more business with you?"

"Are you sure Signor Collins?"

"Of course I'm sure, I think you better make sure that you employ some decent people, your Giorgio has cost me five hundred euro more than I was supposed to pay you, who's going to give me that?"

"If I get hold of him I'll make sure that you'll get your share, as you've been so kind to help me finding out how nasty Giorgio is!"

"Well, I hope you'll get your money alright, would you like me to contact you at the old phone number?"

"Yes please, but don't leave too many details, some of these phones conversation are recorded!"

"Okay, may I tell you that we also record every conversation here at the hotel, in the meantime I'll say bye, bye because I'm wanted on the other line!"

"Bye, bye Mr. Collins and thank you!"

(John put the phone down and said to himself;)
"Whow…I think my blood pressure is gone sky high, now I shall deal with Roberto number two!"

(As he was coming out of his office, coincidence struck twice. Who was coming across the reception? That's alright our friend Roberto, and on its own)
"Hello Roberto, can I trouble you for a few minutes, please, will you be so kind to come into my office? I've got to show you something important!"

"Of course John, no problems, I was just going to the shop to buy a pair of flip flops for my wife!"

"Please take a seat Roberto…. bloody stuffy in here let me open the top window**! (John goes in the far corner a get the long metal stick to open the top little window!"**

"What was it that you wanted to show me John?"
"That's it..... is open now, lovely fresh air...**(John is standing in front of Roberto with his long stick....)**
You know Giorgio five minutes ago I had a phone call from someone called Roberto Tura, and I think he's looking for you, he might arrive in five minutes!"

(As he heard that Giorgio became white as a driven snow, and put his hand in his pocket, but John was quicker and walloped him on his head with his long stick, which made him faint and fell off the chair. John got his hand out of trousers pocket, and yes, he had a gun, which he took and put that away safely in the top draw of his desk, then he started to lift Giorgio up in his chair, that was easy enough as he wasn't a big bloke, gave him a couple of slaps on his face to wake him, but he didn't respond. John started to panic and said to himself; "Christ I killed him!" Touch his pulse and yes poor old Giorgio was dead, So John took his ID which confirmed that he was Giorgio Zucchi and of course he in his pocket nearly a thousand euro, John took all that and put it with his gun, nicely locked up, and started thinking of how to dispose the body. He thought for the moment to put him in his wardrobe which he did, Now he had to deal with the wife, so he went up to his room knocked on the door)
"Sorry to trouble you...is Tina isn't it your name?"
"Yes, what can I do for you? **(With a cigarette in her mouth)**"
"Well, the police just found out that your friend Roberto is called Giorgio Zucchi, who are you Tina? Please tell me the truth, don't tell me that you are his wife, because I can see you are not....okay?"

"Well, you know….I am… one of them…(**Puffing her cigarette**) I only met Roberto the other day, and he ask me if I wanted a free holiday, all I had to do it was to pose as his wife, I really thought it was my lucky day, I said `of course my darling, my name is Tina!"

"How interesting Tina, so you are not husband and wife then, are you?""

"No way, I don't think he's my type, anyway I am married, but separated, the bastard all he wanted it was money to buy his fags and booze."

"Do you have any kids."

"No, thank god for that, I live with my parents now, they look after me when I can't make enough money, it's a hard life to be a prostitute."

But you could get a decent job, then you wouldn't have to walk the streets."

"That's easy said than done, but reality is wages are very low now days and don't forget my parents don't get a good pension, so sometimes I have to help them out!"

"Anyway Tina, I'll have to ask you to leave, unless of course you can afford to pay for the hotel, which I can assure you could cost you quite a few Euros."

"Can't afford that, I suppose you can't offer me a job either. can you?"

"Not really Tina, we are fully staffed, I'll tell you what I'll do though, I should really charge you two hundred euro for today, but since your Roberto, let you down, I can void the charges, but you must promise me that you will not go to the police, because that would mean bad publicity for me, and you might go to prison for assisting a thief."

"Rest assure I wouldn't do that, Mr. John, my parents would kill me if they knew it."

"Right put together your things, and come downstairs, you'll have to sign a piece of paper, which says that you were not able to pay your bill, and the management didn't charge you as a gesture of goodwill."
"You are ever so kind Mr. John thank you very much, if I come across that rascal again I know what I will do."
"Whatever you'll do, I don't think it's worth it!, however he'll be locked up for a long time, that's what the police said"
"Serves him right, he deserves more than that!"

(She signed that paper and said bye, bye to everyone, thanking him again for his kindness, as soon as she went out John called a Luigi the porter)

"Oh..Luigi do us a favour, can you bring to my office a wily-bin and a few big black sacks, as I'm getting rid of some rubbish which is cluttering up my office"!
"Would like me to help[you Mr. Collins?"
"Not really, you have enough on your plate as it is, will you remind me that at ten o/clock I must go to the airport to pick up my ex wife.!
"She's arriving late Mr. Collins!"
"It can be help Luigi, she couldn't get a day flight at all!"

(Luigi brought the wily-bin and the sacks, John started to roll up Giorgio's body which fitted right tin that bin, with some other rubbish on the top, rolled the bin down below in the hotel's garage, put the body in his car boot and locked it up)

Chapter 9

(Back in the office John was looking at Giorgio's gun, only had three bullets in it, but he thought to keep it in his safe, as for the ID that his identity card, which he thought he better destroy it, but he made sure to make a copy of that piece of paper Giorgio signed, just in case it would lose the original. He looked at the map on the road to the airport, and chosen the right spot to dump Giorgio's body right down in the sea, as he really didn't want to throw it on land or rocks and so he found the right spot, and to make sink easily he put in the thick sacks a couple of bricks)

"How's my birthday girl today…Hello Barry hope you look after her, you are older that her!"

"I'm alright thank you, I think you should sunbathe too and some tan on your body uncle!"

"I wish I had the time love, I've got so much on my plate, you wouldn't believe it!"

"What time are you going to pick up Gloria Uncle?"

"I'll probably leave at nine or ten tonight!"

"Can I come? I've never been in your car!"

"No my darling you cannot come, for the simple reason that on my way I must stop to see someone about some business!"

"Never mind uncle, I thought I keep you company, as it quite a long way the airport!"

"Yes it's true, it is a long way, but since I have to stop to see this person, it's just perfect for me. Did you enjoy your birthday last night, Fred was telling me that they surprised you with a cake."

"And a bottle of Prosecco, and then we went into town to have a few drinks, it was really a lovely birthday that everyone gave me, including you Barry."

"Thank you darling I thought you never mention me!"

"So sorry Barry, I blame my uncle, he's such a chatter box, he never let anyone say a word!"

"Now then girl don't blame me, you tell her Barry, stand up for yourself!"

"It's no use John, she's always has the last word!"

"Oh you are funny Barry..ah, ah, ah, ah!"

"I'm going to get a drink Suzanne, would you like one?"

"Yes please Barry I'll have a lemonade!"

(Barry 's gone to get the drinks)

"Suzanne I think you should be more nicer to him really, it's not a bad lad, I see a bright future in you two!"

"Uncle don't make me say something, which you might not like!"

"Alright then, be gentle with him, can't you see he can't take his eyes of you?"

"Yes I know, he keeps looking at my boobs!"

"Ah, ah, ah, ah…Enough of that girl, you behave yourself, just be that nice young lady that I used to know!"

"I know you know me well and what I think of you uncle, pity you won't take me with you at the airport!"

"For goodness sake stop it girl, good job there's no one around us, if they heard you what would they say?"

"Let them think or say what they want, nothing will change my feelings for you!"

"Let's pretend I haven't heard that. Here's he's coming with the drinks, be good darling do it for me!"

"I'll try uncle, and you behave yourself with Gloria, she'll probably eat you alive tonight!"

"Suzanne….Ehm.. see you later the two of you, don't do anything I wouldn't do."

"That'll be a fat chance uncle… not with everybody around us… what do you say Barry?"

"Here…Have your drink and be quite for a moment!"

"Ah, ah, ah! I'll see you later guys!"

"Bye…uncle…"

"Bye, bye John…"

"You seem to like your uncle a lot Suzanne."

"Yes I do Barry, he's been nice to me since I was a little girl, I really consider him like my second dad!"

"That's nice of you to say that, for a minute I thought you fancied him!"

"Don't be silly Barry, is a relation of mine, you don't have love affairs with someone of your family....and that wouldn't be right for a niece to… don't even think of it!"

"Well, it wouldn't be the first time for me to see two relations to fall in love, you know once I even read a story that a brother and sister fell in love!"

"Hard to believe that, I expect you would see that only in films!"

"Yes, but it can happen, don't kid yourself."

"What are you doing tonight Barry?"

"I don't know really, I think I'm getting a bit bored to around with my parents, all they do is sitting around and drinking themselves to death!"

"Yes… I think it's true, me too I'm getting bored sometimes with my parents, I see no excitement in that!"

"Tell you what Suzanne, why can't we go for a walk tonight just us two?"

"Why not Barry, after all we are any longer teenagers, mind you I'll have to ask my parents!"

"What about if they say no, what would you do then?"

"What about you then Barry, what would you say?"

"I don't think they would say no to me Suzanne, after all I am nearly twenty one!"

"I thought you said you were twenty two next!"

"Did I? I don't think so, maybe you misunderstood!"

"Whatever Barry, let's say that we can meet at that coffee bar, and then there and then we'll ask our parents together!"

"Good idea Barry, that way they won't embarrass themselves by refusing us!"

"Right you make sure that you tell your parents that you fancy a drink in that bar…and I shall do the same!"

"Yes Barry that's what we'll do… right I think I'd better go now, and get myself ready for the dinner!"

"You don't need to do yourself up Suzanne, you are beautiful as you are…"

"Barry……!! You naughty boy, behave yourself!"

"See you tonight Suzanne…"

"See you later alligator…ah, ah, ah, ah!"

"Tonight's dinner was really an experience Claire, I never had that sausage with lentils and that yellow puree'!"

"Eddy that was an Italian speciality, on the menu it said Cotecchino and polenta, of course the lentils completed the taste of the whole dish.

"Mind you I wish we had white wine with it, the red one was a bit too dry for me Claire!"

"Oh you are a true English old fashion so and so!"

"What can you do Claire, nothing will change my habits, that's the way I was brought up and I'm proud of it!"

"I'm not complaining about that love. What's your opinion Suzanne?"

"Don't know really, I suppose as we all grow up in different times, we naturally get used to live in different ways!"

"Goodness me you sound like one of the wise men.."

"Thank god I am woman mum....Are we going to that coffee bar later."

"Well, I was thinking to watch some telly tonight, as I had my unusual amount of alcohol last night!"

"Look dad... for a start you won't understand Italian television, then you'll probably fall asleep anyway, for goodness sake snap out of it, we are on holiday."

"She's right you know? You'll have enough time to watch the telly when we go back home!"

"Alright, alright... you win, we'll go for a walk and then we'll stop for a drink, I bet you won't see Fred tonight, as I think he had enough last night!"

"I bet you he'll be there, he know how to enjoy his life and so does Laura.."

"That was a lovely walk Claire, it helped my digestion, that sausage was a bit too rich for me, now I need a nice brandy!"

"That's what I like to hear dad, you just enjoy yourself!"

"And I think I shall have a crème de menthe with lots of ice and a straw."

"Lemonade for me as usual, I do fancy some champagne but nobody is offering….."

"Listen to her she thinks we are millionaires , where did we leave our yacht princess?"

"Down at the docks mum……Look who's coming. See? I told you they would come!"

"Maybe you arranged it Suzanne."

"Perhaps I did mum…"

"Hello everyone…Just about to order some drinks, what would you like folks…."

"It's my turn Eddy…I'll get them…."

"Oh no you won't Fred you done enough last night!"

"Well… thank you Eddy, we shall drink to your good health…"

"And yours too Fred...... Cheers Laura…"

"While you enjoy your drinks, do you mind if Suzanne and I go for a short walk?"

"Excuse me Barry, I think you should ask me not my parents…."

"I only ask your parents for their permission, and of course I will ask my parents too, hope they don't mind!"

"Go on son, you don't need to ask us, just ask Suzanne!"

"Yes Susanne?"

"Why not Barry, let the young generation enjoy their drinks!"

"Cheeky so and so…. and don't be late you two!"

"Yes don't be late Barry, make sure you keep an eye on that lovely girl!"

"More likely she'll keep an eye on him!"

"You are probably right Laura!"

"Cheers Eddy and to you Claire, and of course our lovely children, not to forget my lovely Laura, who's the best of all my family!"

"That's a lovely speech Fred, thank you....What are you after?!"
"I will let you know later darling!"
"Do you get that too Claire?"
"Yes… mind you I don't hear him saying that a lot!"
"Thank you dear....I shall remember that!"

(In the meantime John was leaving the hotel, to pick up Gloria at the airport. Half an hour later he arrived at spot where he planned to get rid of Giorgio's body, he parked the car right near the cliff, got out and looked left and right, nobody seemed to around, took out his sack from the boot put it near the cliff, looked around again and with a strong push he rolled it down the bottom of the cliff, which made quite a splash in the waters below. Got in his car and made his way to the airport, and mumble to himself;) "Bloody good riddance to old trash!"

Chapter 10

(Suzanne and Barry were having a walk on the beach and holding hands, strange enough, he was very happy, because he enjoyed so much her way of talking, that he even thought that he could learn something from her)

"Susanne sometime I wonder why you haven't got a boyfriend, or shall I say you never had one!"

"Well Barry...I'll be honest with you, it never bothered me, maybe that has something to do the way I was brought up, not that I don't like boys, on the contrary, I'm very orientated on the opposite sex."

"I presume you are waiting to come across the right one,"

"Perhaps Barry, but there again when I come across someone I like I find he never likes me!"

"That is sad and very unfortunate, you know I like you very much Suzanne but sometime I've got the feeling that you discourage me to like you!"

"Not really Barry, I think that's all in your mind, or perhaps you are not sure of yourself!"

"Maybe you are right, sometime when I look at you....You know, I can't explain it.... Yes I know I can't take my eyes of you, you are so different than other girls I know."

"I've notice that, You stare at my body, as if you have never seen any other, of course a woman likes that, as it is our beauty that makes men interested, but from a woman side, there are other things that makes her interested!"

"Suzanne you are confusing me, dam it not only you are beautiful but also intelligent, you can get around subjects that never came across my mind, you know I could kiss you for that!"

You see that's another point of getting a female interested, you don't say I could kiss you, things like that we say it to little babies!"

"Once again I flopped, what is the recipe then?"

(Suzanne grabbed his hand very tight and...)

"For goodness sake Barry, look in my eyes, if I see I look into yours, just kiss me, and whisper sweet nothing, and don't look for….. food yet….work on it!"

(Yes….he did just that and kissed her, obviously she responded, which lasted a few minutes)

"Gosh Suzanne I think I love so much, you drive me crazy!"

"What do you mean you think? Barry you just did that because I told you so, and of course I am attracted to you!"

"Yes…. Yes… I think we better walk back, I'm sure our parents are already in bed!"

"Of course Barry…You know I really enjoyed our walk..!"

"And I really enjoyed your lesson in love, I find you very interesting, I could listen you talking all night!"

"You know something Barry, I feel exhausted, maybe it's time for bed…."

"Is that a promise Suzanne?"

"I think you got the wrong hand of the stick..ah, ah, ah!"

"I did not mean what you thought…Ah, ah, ah, ah!"

(Barry took Suzanne back to her Hotel, right to the entrance door)

"Goodnight Suzanne and thank you once again, I really did enjoy your company, we must do it again." **(And kissed her on her cheek)**
"Of course Barry, it was really lovely...Good night, see you tomorrow down at the pool!"

(John was now at the airport waiting for Gloria and speak of the devil there she was coming out of the arrivals doors)

"Hello sweetheart, did you have a good flight?"
"Yes John, a really pleasant one, pity it was at this time of the night. from the previous ones, during the day that is, were so much better, as I loved to watch chain of Dolomites full of snow!"
"Surely they haven't got snow this time of the year the Dolomites."
"Of course they have, some of them mountains have snow all year around!"
"Anyway Gloria, how's everyone at home? Your parents are alright I hope!"
"Oh they are fine and they send their regards!"
"I hope they didn't say that usual sentence that I really don't like, especially from your mum, and yet I still like her very much!"
"No...She didn't say; why do you bother with him, I just don't know! Is that one?"
"That's it Gloria, what a memory you've got, of course she said it so many times, a few times she said it to my face!"

"Can we leave that in the past John? Now I am here and I want to enjoy my week, after all it cost me a fortune!"

"Maybe Gloria, but don't forget that, your staying and food it's on me too!"

"That'll be the day....you mean on the hotel patron!"

"Not so much, it will come out of my yearly bonus, already my brother and family cost me a little packet when they arrived! Good job they are staying in another hotel."

"Oh...You are so mean sometime, you mean to tell me that you would begrudge a little hospitality to you own family?"

"I didn't mean that Gloria, you know I would do anything for my family!"

"Yes I know that, deep down you are not too bad...This road is very bumpy John."

"Don't worry soon we'll take the motorway, I took this road because it was much quicker."

"Knowing you...Just thinking of saving some petrol!"

"Did you bring that money Gloria?"

"Yes of course darling, would I forget it?"

"Just asking....Jus asking!"

"So how did that accident occurred?"

"I park my car in particular car park, there were no cars either sides, when I returned I could barely get into my car, I really squeezed myself in, and as I was reversing I knocked it's side and bumper, because it wasn't a scratch but a dent, this chap insisted that it would cost two thousand euro, I said it would not be that much, but half of it, he said I had a choice to through my insurance, in that case the police would have been involved!"

"Why didn't you ask your insurance to pay for it?"

"Gloria I told you already that when I looked at my insurance, I noticed that it expired two days before!"

"Oh yes now I remember you mentioned that on the phone!"

"So if the police came, I really would have been in trouble, as you know in my position I cannot afford to have such problem, if they locked me up I would have lost my job too!"

"I understand John, Am I right to say that you were an assistant manager before?"

"Yes Gloria, the previous General Manager had some problems with the fraud drug squad police!"

"Blamey that was bad, how did they find he was involved in such terrible doing?"

"Well…one evening he was driving to some friends home, when he was stopped by these nasty lot, they search his car and they found cocaine in his bonnet!"

"Did the police knew he had drugs?"

"No…I think it was the usual searching routine, in Italy happens quite a lot, as there are many trafficking drugs, anyway to cut the story short, he lost his job and I've got a promotion as a General Manager with my private little chalet, if you like to stay there tonight you are welcome!"

"No John..That's kind of you but I rather stay in my bedroom, I hope you got me a nice one, and not one in the attic, I wouldn't past you!"

"Come Gloria who you take me for?"

"Well, sometimes I think why do I bother to stay friend with you."

"Now you are being very unfair, after all I treated you alright when we were together….True?"

"Yes you did, and we would still be together if you didn't bedded that tart, have you seen her lately?"

"I haven't seen her for ages, anyway, she is in England!"

"Of course she is in England, maybe if she was here you'd do the same…Wouldn't you..be honest!"

"No way darling, I learned my lesson, and thanks to her , I lost the one, who sadly I regret and I never stopped loving, of course that's you!"

"My god... you know how to talk to a lady John, I can say that you will never be without one, I see we are arrived now. Good lord that is big, how many bedrooms?"

"Around Five hundred and fifty!"

"That's a lot to be responsible for...what a headache!"

(John signed her in and took her up to her bedroom)
"That's nice John, and thank you for putting me on the first floor, I hate lifts, that is, since I was in that big department store, and the lift stopped half way, that was an experience I tell you!"

"I remember that Gloria…You nearly s…..yourself!"

"I'm glad you never finished that word…I hate it!"

"Gloria, if you are hungry I will send you up a sandwich, there you have tea or coffee and biscuits!"

"No I'm not hungry John many thanks, I've had something on the plane, right….I'll see you tomorrow then John…"

"Oh Gloria do you think I could have that envelope, so tomorrow morning I'll pop it over to this chap!"

"There you are naughty boy, they are all there!"

Many thanks Gloria, I promise I will pay you back very soon, this job is gratifying me well!"

"I hope you will John….Good night."

"Good night darling…(**Kissing her on her cheek)**

(In the meantime Suzanne was undressing for bed when her mother knocked at the door….)

"Thank god you are home, we've been worried sick about you, where did you go?"

"Mum… what were you worrying about, we only went for a walk around town then we ended down on the beach, we started talking and talking in no time at all we realized that it was quite late, sorry about that Mum!"

"Okay darling..don't worry, just for the fact your father was worried sick too, now he's gone off to sleep. No wonder after those couple of brandies he had!"

"Well, I hope he did enjoy himself, he deserve it after all the work he does all year around, and you should enjoy yourself a bit, and stop worrying about me, I am eighteen now."

"Alright darling but you must know that us parents always worry about you, sleep tight Suzanne, we'll see you at breakfast!"

""Good night mum… you sleep tight too!"

Chapter 11

(next morning at breakfast, the atmosphere was quite thick, no one seemed to say much, except pass the toasts)

"I'm going to the swimming pool dad is that alright?"
"I don't see why not, you spent nearly all night out last night, perhaps you ought to know that we were worried sick, knowing that we are in a different country!"
"Dad… Being in a different country, doesn't make any difference, bad things happen in our country too…You are making a drama out of nothing, supposing I was going on holiday with a friend of mine, would you be worried just the same…considering you two not being there?"
"Well.. That would be different, because at least we would know that you would be there, with your friend."
"It is the same thing dad, I don't see any difference at all."
"For goodness sake will you stop you two, I can see people over there watching and listen your stupid show!"
"Sorry Claire, maybe I'm exaggerating a bit, probably because I love you so much Suzanne."
"Thank you father, so will you please stop being so possessive?"

"I don't think I am Suzanne, as I said before I do and act like this because I love you very much!"

"So do you think I should wait until I'll be twenty one to have a bit of freedom?"

"Not necessarily darling, may I remind you that we have given you quite a bit of freedom, so far, and to prove that, we haven't locked you up…..Yet…ah, ah, ah, ah!"

"Perhaps you think that was funny dad, yes, I know you both worry when I go out somewhere and come back at the wrong time, but please, please, try to get used to it!"

"What do you think Claire/"

"Yes I think we should try and give her a bit more credit!"

"Thank you, I love you both, and now I shall go to the hotel swimming pool. What are you going to do today and where are you going? After all if I don't know where you are and when you'll be back, I will be worried sick!"

"Now then Suzanne, you are being a bit sarcastic, you just behave yourself."

"See what I mean. Why should you be the only ones to worry?"

"Go on go and enjoy yourself at the pool."

(Meanwhile at the open restaurant near the pool, Gloria is having her first breakfast.)

"Good morning darling , did you sleep well?"

"Oh… good morning John, yes thank you, that was a very comfortable bed, and shower is magnificent. Have you been up early?"

"Oh yes, I get up at six every morning, and check various departments, to that the day starts off nicely and I went to pay off my debt, so that is one less problem in my life!"

"I understand your feeling and I bet you've been worried sick…..Will you sit and have coffee with me?"

"I'm afraid not now darling, I'm holding a staff meeting this morning and then we'll have a fire drill!"

"I suppose it's not easy to be in charge of a Hotel of this size, how many staff do you have?"

"In full season we have more than sixty, when is quiet we run it with forty..**(John's phone rung)** Hello, who is it? alright I'll be there in a second....!"

"Any problem John?"

"I don't know, the reception tells me a police inspector wants to see me!"

"Good morning Mr. Collins, how are you? I won't take much of your time I promise you!"

"I'm well thank you....No problem Ispettore….."

"Here's my credentials, my name is Ispettore Lancini…."

"What can I do for you Ispettore?"

"Well.. it's about Mr. Luca Vanni your previous manager, I'm pleased to say that after various tests, we have come to the conclusion that he never took any drugs at all, and also we certain that he never dealt with them either…!"

"I am very pleased to hear that Inspector!"

"Actually we think that someone had planted that cocaine in his bonnet, do you know anyone who could have done something like that?"

"Well, to be honest Inspector, Luca and I were like two brothers, never argued about anything, and then of course I couldn't think of anyone who really disliked him, in saying so, when you have a top position there's always someone who would stubs you on the back."

"Yes I do understand what you mean Mr. Collins, anyway here's my card, if you suspect or think of anyone, please let us know, however, I'm sure you'll be pleased to know that Mr. Vanni has found now a similar job."

"I am so pleased to hear that, more than anything I wish him well in his new job, if you see him please convey my best wishes."

"Yes of course, and thank you for your help!"

"I am delighted to have been able to assist you, I'm sorry I couldn't do more."

"Goodbye Mr. Collins."

"Goodbye Inspector Lancing!"

(As soon as the Inspector left, John sat down and…..)

"Bloody hell…. I think I better have a double brandy."

"Good morning Barry, how are you this morning did you have any problems last night with your parents?"

"Not really Suzanne. Why did you?"

"Not so much last night, but this morning my dad wasn't very happy, so we had a little friendly argument!"

"For goodness sake Suzanne, you are eighteen now, you should tell your parents that they are back in the dark ages."

"So true, in the eastern countries a girl would stand a chance to out late at night with a fellow, of course us in the continent we are more up to date."

"Not every family, my one yes."

"Don't forget that you are boy, and is different for you, on the other hand my parents are a little bit strict on those matter!"

"Of course I don't blame them, they know that they have a beautiful daughter and she can be kidnap anytime."

"Let them try, they don't know me at all, I've done a bit of judo, not that I gained the black belt, but I know how to defend myself!"

"So I better behave myself, just in case you send me to hospital!"

"Hello Suzanne...Surprise, surprise, so nice to see you again, my god you are sun tanned and it suits you well!"

"Hello Gloria, nice to see you too, I knew you were coming uncle John told yesterday!"

"Yes he picked me up last night at the airport...How's your parents, I am looking forward to see them and have a little chat with your mum, I haven't seen her for ages!"

"Oh...they are fine, and I'm sure they are looking forward to you too, incidentally, I told my mum that I met you at the hairdresser."

"I bet she was surprise...Are you going to introduce me to your friend?"

"This is Barry, actually he is almost our neighbor in England, he's here with parents and they live in Littlewood."

"Fancy that...I have quite a few relatives living there, what a coincidence, nice to meet you Barry... and I don't want to be nosey Suzanne, are you and Barry....Yes?

"No...Nothing like that Gloria, we are just good friends, anyway we only met a week ago!"

"It's true Gloria, hope you don't mind me being familiar by just calling you Gloria."

"Not at all Barry, actually you made me feel young, or shall I say part of your new generation!"

(In that moment John appeared instantly)

"Lovely to see that you are all chatting happily, so you met each other alright."

"Yes, Suzanne introduced me to Barry too!"

"Yes uncle, we seemed to have know each other for years, and so happy to see Gloria here with you, you know something Barry, I really don't see any arm at all to stay friends when you break up, in fact it's lovely, life is too short to bear grudges...Unlike what I told you before."

"My god you've got a clever niece John, and really up to date, yes of course Suzanne, John and I remained very good friends, sad really that sometimes you feel the loneliness, but in saying that you gain the freedom, which it is very important in life!"

"Now Suzanne, don't believe everything she says, I always thought she should have been a lawyer!"

"Have you sorted out that problem al right John?"

"Yes that was nothing really, just wanted to details about a customer, that paid with a cheque and subsequently it bounced, why people would behave like that I don't know, you only have to keep a good eye on your bank account!"

"I presume you are very careful with your financial situation."

"Of course I am Gloria...**(the phone rings again)** This phone never stop ringing....Hello Yes I'll be there in a minute....Duty calls again...see you later."

"There's a disco tonight in the hotel Gloria, will you be attending? Suzanne and I will be there!"

"I don't know, maybe I shall have dinner with John tonight!"

"Well??.....I didn't know I was going Barry, it would be nice if I was asked!"

"Sorry Susanne, I thought you knew that,"

"Yes I knew that, but I didn't know I was going with you!"

"So sorry Suzanne… will you come to the disco tonight?"

"Of course I will darling, and you Gloria, please try to come too, I enjoy so much talking to you, I really wish you would have stayed as an aunty as you were when you married John."

"Yes I wish he behaved better, perhaps we would still be together, you know that I still love him Suzanne!"

"Yes I can tell that aunty Gloria…ah, ah, ah, ah!"

"Don't worry you can carry on calling me aunty for ever if you wish..."

"I think I will aunty... thank you very much!"

Chapter 12

(After dinner they met up in the vast ballroom, where the disco was taking place that evening)

"Gosh you are really good mover Barry, where did you learn to dance like that?"

"My teacher taught me, after school I used to visit her, she used to live very near our house, funny girl she was!"

"Really… and old was she then?"

"I never asked her, I think she was maybe over twenty five, she liked to talk about intimate things."

"like what for instance?"

"She wanted to know if I fantasize about girls, you know?"

"Yes I can imagine Barry, maybe she did like young boys."

"Come to think of it she used to hold me very tight when we danced the old ballroom dance.!

"You mean the tango?"

"That's alright the tango, of course I was only sixteen then and I was a bit green in certain things, but when I think now, I think she must have found some pleasure out of that!"

"And you…did you feel anything?"

"Of course I did, but I was too afraid to do something that would cause an outcry, with her and then my parents, when I think of I really missed something there...Yes the more I think about that, the more I'm convinced that she fancied me!"

"Poor old Barry, now I suppose, you find it difficult to come across such beautiful occasions!"

"It's not very easy, that's for certain, I suppose I'm a bit shy when I come to commit myself with some girls, they might think I am a pervert!"

"You are more a pervert if you stare at a girl's boobs, I noticed that you do that to me now and then!"

"I'm sorry Suzanne, but you look so beautiful and of course sexy, I can see you like men and not girls!"

"I could say you are right there Barry, like some men fancy men, some girls fancy girls.."

"Did you come across one of them too Suzanne?"

"Yes, I remember I must have been seventeen then an I was in the job just for a few months, there I was in the ladies as I was washing my hands, this girl came in, she was a part-timer, she was the same age as me I think, as I was drying my hands, she grab the towel I was holding she pull me toward herself and kissed me and she said; every time I look at you turn me on!"

"Did you say anything to that?"

"Of course I did, I looked at her and I laughed, and said; thank you for the compliment, if you do that once more I'll report you to the boss!"

"What did she say to that Suzanne?"

"She apologized and never again she put a finger on me!"

"What a lovely story, I suppose when we were at that age we all had some funny stories to tell!"

"I suppose you are right Barry... Look at the two new lovers, shall we go and split them..."

"Why not Suzanne... you say something to them as your more attached as a niece!"

"Come then you two, let us try your dancing expertise!"

"Oh alright Suzanne, I was enjoying that, you know I don't remember the time and when Gloria and I dance together!"

"Come here you... young Barry, I show you what I can do!"

"Oh yes...how's that for a starter..Miss Gloria!"

"Goodness me Barry, you surely can move fast.."

"That's nothing if you could see me, how good I do the slow ones!"

"Oh yes.. you mean the tango? I like people who take their time, it's more enjoyable!"

"That's nice to hear Gloria...!"

(And so Gloria and Barry seemed to get truly acquainted, as for Suzanne and John seemed to take more easy as they started to chat away)

"I can see some of your staff are looking at you, actually I noticed that you have quite a few pretty girls working here and in the restaurant!"

"True Suzanne, I find girls are much better workers that boy and faster!"

"I see that blond over there that she hasn't taken her of you, I can see she fancies you!"

"Don't be silly Suzanne, even so I would never dear to.. I could lose my job...... you know?"

"Yes I suppose you are right, and I would be very annoyed, more than that I think.... very jealous."

"You stop that Suzanne, one of these days you are going to get me in trouble with my brother, just the thought of it makes me shiver."

"You make me shiver when you touch me, please hold me tight for a few seconds uncle!"

"Good lord, please don't ask me to do that here? Look Gloria is not very far, and Barry is looking at you!"

"First of all Gloria is not married to you any longer and Barry is looking at me and my boobs all day long, I told him a couple of times to stop it in a sort of way."

"What do you mean in a sort of way Suzanne? And yes Gloria and I are not married, but she still feels something for me, and perhaps I still feel something for her"

"I understand that uncle, but let me tell you that you will never love her again like you used to and as for Barry, I try to make him understand that it's not nice to stare like he does as girls might think he's a pervert!"

"Darling can we go and sit down for a while, these new dancing makes me rather tired!"

"It's not the dancing, it's your age uncle…ah, ah, ah, ah!"

"You tell him Suzanne, he's getting an old man!"

"Thank you Gloria, if you think that a thirty year old man is getting old, what about the seventy ones then ?"

"They are finished, but they are rewarded by reaching that age, whom very few and far get there!"

"Well, thank god I've got something to look forward then, right I think I'm having one more drink and then I will retire to my quarters!"

"Would you like me to come and turn down the bed sheets uncle, that is if Gloria don't want to do that!"

"Not really Suzanne, anyway I think his chambermaid already done that, am I right John?"

"Yes I think you are Gloria, but I would have liked you to do that, like old times!"

"Now, now then, am I detecting an offer is on the cards?"

"He should be so lucky Suzanne…."

"Please Gloria...I guess you don't know what you are missing!"
"Please will you stop you two?"

(Gloria and Suzanne looked at each other and burst out laughing, Barry did likewise)
"Well, how about me then what am I suppose to do?"
"Alright Barry you can come and turned down my sheets!"
"Thank you Gloria, as much as I would but I don't think the hotel management would appreciate that!"
"Absolutely right Barry, you might be right on that but you are too inexpert to do that!"
"Ah.... well then, I think I have no choice but to join my parents, I think they are in the other bar with Suzanne's parents!"
"I'll come with you Barry, leave the young lovers on their own, please remember we don't want to see any human productions!"
"That's very funny Suzanne, I think your uncle is just running out of luck."
"I hope you mean that Gloria, does it deserve that?"
"Little sweetheart I thought you were on my side, how can I win back what I want if I have enemies around me?"
"I'm sorry uncle, but so far I tried my best, but it looks like you are out of favours!"
"In that case I bid you goodnight all, and thank you for the lovely evening. Come on Gloria let us have on for the road, in my private bar."
"Okay darling....if you insist!"
"Goodnight the both of you**...**"**(Blowing him a kiss)**
"Goodnight Suzanne, Goodnight Barry...."

"Hello parents… still discussing the world affairs?"
"I think we said far too much Suzanne, I'm going to bed Fred, are you coming Claire?"
"Go on Claire, show the way to you sweetheart!"
"Of course I'm coming darling, I don't want you to lose your way along the street, easy for these three they don't have far to go!"
"Goodnight Suzanne, it has been a lovely evening, I enjoyed dancing with you…soooo much!"
"Me too Barry…Goodnight..see you tomorrow!"
"Goodnight all, and bless you…"
"Come on Eddy… hold my hand…"

(Meanwhile Gloria and John were having their last drink in the pool bar)

"Cheers Gloria, and thank you for coming to see me, I am so happy that you are here, it feels almost like the old times..you know what I mean darling?"
"Yes I do know what you mean John, but supposing we get back together again…will it work?"
"Darling it can only work if we work it out together, it won't work on its own!"
"I don't know if it is the drink that makes me think that you are telling the truth, in any case, we can always have a try, but a single of your escapades, nothing will save you from decapitation, this time!"
"Do you mean you will cut my head off!"
"Not that head plonker but your lower head, and to that I will drink with pleasure!"
"I hope you don't mean that love, I'm getting the shivers already..Christ… one of my best possessions!"

"So you better behave yourself darling… don't wake me when you get up in the morning!"

"I'll do my best darling, come on then, let's go to bed, I fancy a soothing night…."

"What time are you supposed to get in the morning?"

"Very early Gloria, but you can stay as long as you like, you are on holiday..."

"And you are working John.... I know...I can see you are closing your eyes already!"

"No I am not, what makes you think that?"

"Nothing makes me think that...I just can see it!"

"Good lord I really feel tired........Gloria...."

Chapter 13

(John was up early and right behind the reception desk, checking the new arrivals)

"Hello Jean, how many arrivals have we got this morning"?

"I think about a dozen families Mr. Collins!"

"As they cannot move into their rooms before two pm, make sure they'll have a proper breakfast....Okay?"

"Of course Mr. Collins…"

"Here we go again **(His phone rings)** Hello… who's that? of course hold on a minute….. Jean I will take this call in my office okay? Put it through my private line!"

"Yes Mr Collins…"

"Hello Mr. Collins is that you… this is Roberto Tura…"

"Yes it's me Mr. Tura, what can I do for you at this early time in the morning!"

"I'm sorry I thought I call you early so I can catch you, without interruptions!"

"Fair enough Mr. Tura.. speak up…"

"I read in the newspaper that they found Giorgio, did the police contact you?"

"Yes, Ispettore Lancini was here yesterday, asking me If I knew him, as they found a brochure of the hotel in his little pocket, but that's all they found, I wonder where my money and yours went!"

"Yes I was wondering too, maybe he had spent it already, but I don't really care about that, what I care is that I don't want the police to find out that Giorgio was connected with my organization."

"You are lucky Mr. Tura because I never told the Inspettore that he was working for you, but he said that he might come back and ask me more questions!"

"I tell what I will do for you Mr. Collins, I decided that I will refund you the money you lost, on top I will give you something extra, all I want is that you keep your mouth shut, are you agreeing?"

"That's quite acceptable, in a way if I had told the Ispettore that Giorgio fiddled me, I certainly wouldn't have said drugs, but maybe a small motorbike, of course Giorgio couldn't have contested this as he's dead, so how much you intend to refund me to keep my mouth shut?"

"I will give you a thousand euro, I will send someone with a little envelope sometime today!"

"Will you require a receipt Mr. Tura?"

"I'm afraid yes, just to make sure that you get it, and not my messenger boy, I came to the conclusion that I don't even trust, members of my family!"

"Thank you Mr. Tura…bye, bye."

"Bye, bye.. Mr. Collins!"

(Meanwhile at the hotel Sea View Suzanne and family were having their breakfast)

"Suzanne dad and I thought to go in town today to buy a few present for your grandparents, would you like to come? You might see something for yourself too!"

"I think it's a good idea mum, I can go to the pool this afternoon."

"Did you enjoy the disco last night, I see you were dancing like I don't know what!"

"Yes I did enjoy myself, I hadn't dance like that for ages, ands Barry is a good dancer….You know?"

"Your uncle John is good too, we noticed you dancing with him, rather close, I'd say!"

"What are you saying mum? That must have been a tango, that's the way it should be danced!"

"If you say so dear…"

"Mum..sometime you are so old fashioned, honestly, you and dad really are and for that matter I was even danced close with Barry too."

"I didn't notice that as we were sitting on the other side then!"

"Honestly mum you are very suspicious."

"I am sorry my dear, you must understand us parents think the impossible sometimes!"

"Has dad mentioned something about that?"

"No… it was just me, anyway forget I said that and let's get ready for our shopping!"

"Okay mum, let's forget it!"

(They enjoyed their shopping and bought quite a few presents, and some something for themselves, and they even stopped for a pre lunch drink at the usual coffee bar)

"Lovely this campari Claire, I've never tried it before, I don't think you would like it, as it tastes quite bitter!"

"No I don't think I would try it, I quite fond of sweet sherry, that's about it."

"You should try other drinks mum, be a little bit more adventurous you must follow the times, the British have been stuck with their fish and chips for hundreds of years until they realized that the continent were enjoying themselves better."

"You are exaggerating Suzanne…"

"No I am not mum, just look around, does this place look like an English northern or western holiday towns? All you can eat there is pie and mash swimming in thick gravy!"

"Yes I think you've got a point there, last time we went to blackpost, the hotel was dirty and their food was atrocious, alright it was a bit cheaper than where we are now, but I must say it is better!"

"I think Suzanne is right in quite a few things, for instance there's no way, but the French cooking is first class too!"

"Anyway…You must have spent quite a lot mum, by the look of your bags!"

"Yes she did, good job we are not flying, otherwise it would cost a fortune in luggage weight."

"Yes dad and it's so much better by car, you see more all the beautiful views along the way!"

"Mind you in saying that it is more expensive, when you consider that we have to stop a couple of times in hotels."

"So what dad, for goodness sake, you and mum haven't had a proper holiday for a long time, you should enjoy yourselves more, now that I am grown up!"

"You've got a point there darling, we can't take those few savings with us."

"Don't worry mum, you can leave with me, I'll find a way to spend them!"

"Cheeky so and so, come on then let's go back to our hotel for lunch!"

"See mum? as I was saying before, in England you wouldn't find a choice of food like this, unless of course you would go in a five star hotel!"

"Yes darling, I did say you had a point."

"Thank you…Do you mind if I go back to the pool after lunch mum?"

"Not at all, unless you want to come down to the beach with us!"

"For goodness sake Claire, let her go to the pool, Barry will be happy to see her and have a good swim!"

"I was just suggesting Eddy!"

"I don't mind… which ever…"

"No you where you want to go, and we go where we want to go, how's that for fairness?

"Thank you…I love you both!"

(Suzanne ten minutes later was at the pool)

"Hi Barry…Fancy a swim?

"Hi Suzanne.. what a question, of course darling!"

(Twenty minutes later they both lay in the sun)
"Here Suzanne, don't laugh, this morning I had breakfast with Gloria, and I said without thinking; did you have a nice sleep last night? She replied; You mean he had a nice sleep, he nearly didn't undressed, and he was asleep!"

"Maybe he's had too many drinks last night, I asked!"

"Far too many Barry, she said, he was a little tipsy when we walk down to his Chalet! Never mind Gloria, I replied, he'll make up for it tonight..! Again she said…No chance Barry, tonight I'm going in my own bed!"

"I bet he wasn't very happy this morning!"

"I guess not Suzanne, how about you did you sleep well?"

"No problems…I always sleep like a log! And you Barry?"

"Likewise Suzanne…Another three days and then we shall go home, you'll have another five, if I'm not mistaken!"

"That's alright Barry, I'll be lonely without you here!"

"Don't say silly things, your beauty will captivate hundred of males!"

"I don't know so much, yes, I think I will really miss you!"

"Thank you for the compliment Suzanne, as a matter of fact, there's something I want to ask you..but…!"

"What stopping you?"

"Knowing you I never know what you are going to answer!"

"Come on don't be shy…"

"Well….it's like this, I think, not only thinking but, when we are both in England…anyway I want to go out with you, I do enjoy your company…and yes I like you very much, and don't say again that I've fallen in love with your body…"

"Actually I noticed that you haven't looked at my body that much today, for a moment I thought you gone off of me!"

"You are joking of course Suzanne!"

"No I am serious, and yes of course we'll see each other and go out a few times, because I like you too Barry!"

(Grabbing his hand and kissing him gently, making him blush)

"I think I better have a swim, I need cooling down.."

"Ah, ah, ah I'll come with you Barry….!"

(Meanwhile John was walking by the reception)
"Mr. Collins, someone left this envelope for you, the delivery chap made me sign, to make sure you get it!"
"Thank you Jean, much oblige, **(He open it and there was the thousand euro from Roberto Taro)** That's what I like to see….Honesty… thought to himself!"

"Hello John…You seem to be pleased for yourself, have you won at the lottery?"
"You might say that, and my winning is you darling, oh, I know what I was going to tell you…."
"Go on story teller.."
"No need to be nasty darling, but I just want to apologize about last night, by falling with the angels, you know something, I don't even remembering falling asleep!"
"I do remember well, and I was awake half of the night listening to your snoring!"
"So sorry about that darling, I promise I'm going to make it up to you, how about tonight?"
"I don't know darling… let me think about it."
"There's no need to be like that Gloria…"
"I'll see you later in the bar for a drink John!"
"Shall look forward to that…Sweetheart….."

Chapter 14

"Oh..Luigi there some luggage to transfer to room 434 from 233, would see that is done please?"

"Right away Mr Collins, is there anything else you want me to do before I go off duty?"

"No that'll be alright Luigi, you go and enjoy your couple days off, if I need help Remo will be at hand."

"Thank you sir!"

(Suzanne jus coming out of the ladies)

"Hi uncle.. how are you feeling today?"

"I feel alright, what a silly question darling, why are you asking me that?"

"Well, I thought you had a glass more than usual last night, if you don't mind me saying so!"

"I did indeed, but now I recovered completely... goodness me you look very red, well I should think burned on your back, I think you should put some cream to sooth it!"

"To be honest I run out of it, I was going to buy some this morning in town, but I forgot!"

"Come here you trouble, I've got something in my office, let's go and get it!"

(The office was just across the reception, so they went in)

"Let me put it on darling , I'll be very gentle…**"(and so he rubbed the cream onto her back and she started to breathe heavily)** "please uncle, more please…she whispered" **(and before he knew it, she turned around and she kissed him passionately, the touch of their lips was like an electric shock for both of them, that lasted for a couple of minutes)**

"Susanne we shouldn't do this, you know it's wrong!"

"You seemed to have enjoyed it too uncle, please don't tell me to stop pestering you, I think I've fallen in love with you, I just couldn't stand seeing you with Gloria last night, you held her so tight when you were dancing!"

"But Suzanne… after all she's my wife!"

"You mean ex wife, and I'm glad that you didn't make love to her last night!"

"Flipping hell, how do you know that?"

"Barry told me, Gloria was talking to him this morning and said that you fell asleep even before you got undressed!"

"That's bloo…..y unfair, that woman makes me mad sometime, she's so flipping demanding!"

"It's your fault, you are to blame for it, you should have got the right woman."

"Mind you, it was a bit my fault as well, you see if that woman who pestered me for quite a long time, didn't do that, I wouldn't have fallen into her net, no she had to do that, and by misfortune Gloria caught us in bed.

"How did Gloria knew about your relation with that woman and what was her name then?"

"Her name was Vicky, she was quite pretty, but not very clever, all she wanted is to get someone so she would get a home to live in!"

"So, she was a money-taker, she would never have enough."

"Yes she was, but it didn't work out right for her, and of course I realized that too late…"

"Of course that caused the divorce."

"Yes, but don't worry I got rid of her soon after, I was sad to lose Gloria because…."

"Yes, because the family was quite well off, you silly sod!"

"You can say that again, but please you and I it's just not right, although I do like you, you are beautiful, clever, and very mature, what else can a man ask in life?"

"Mind you I haven't any money to offer you, so you'll have to provide that!"

"That's not a problem, I've got a gift of the gab, and I can adapt myself to do any jobs that comes around!"

"You know what my mother said this morning John?"

"Please don't tell me… go on what did she say?"

"She said that she noticed that you and I were dancing too close to each other!"

"Flipping hell, not another problem, did she really?"

"Yes, I said we were dancing a tango, which it was, and that is the way it should be danced!"

"I managed to convince her, and that was it, but I must say though, I love my parents very much, but sometime they treat me like a twelve year old girl!"

"I tell you why Suzanne, it's because you are the only child and they are so afraid to lose you, for some stupid mistakes!"

"Maybe so John, but I am a woman now and I feel like a woman, and I like the opposite sex!"

"Don't I know, but I suppose it's normal, you could have fallen in love with another men for that matter, unfortunate for you that you are convinced that you fancy me!"

"I am not convinced, I truly love you, there's something about you that turn me on!"

"I think you better go back to the swimming pool before the reception start think, something they shouldn't!"

"Okay I'm going now and don't you dare to go to bed with Gloria tonight!"

"What if we already arranged it?"

"Cancel it... tell her you've got headache or something like that, perhaps have a few more drinks, they will help you to go to sleep!"

"Go on darling, and don't stay too long in the sun!"

"I'll see you later uncle and thank you for the cream!"

(Barry was getting quite edgy)

"Good lord I thought you went back to your hotel Suzanne."

"I nearly did Barry, I felt a bit burning on my back, and ask my uncle if he had some soothing cream, as I forgot to buy it this morning."

"You better stay in the shade then, I think I will do the same as I feel a little bit burned on my legs."

"Oh.... I never asked you what kind of work you do by following your father business Barry, what do you do?"

"I do a bit of everything but my main passion is to lay bricks, I can now lay almost five hundred bricks in one hour, that's quite a record."

"Who taught you to do that?"

"I just watched our workers... some of them are really fast!"

"Didn't you want to go to university, I'm sure your parents could afford that!"

"I could have gone if I wanted to, but my dad said it was a waste of time, he said as long as you can read and write the rest comes along naturally, how about you then, why didn't you go to university?"

"Because my parents couldn't afford to, anyway I always like to learn to be an hairdresser, and I love it!"

"You see Suzanne, some of my friends, little older than me, they went to university, and then they struggle to find a job, much easier if you learn a trade!"

"That's true Barry, I've only worked there for about three years and already I had three offers from other hairdressers."

"See what I mean? Good for you!"

"My tummy is rumbling Suzanne I think I'm going to have an hamburger, do you want one and a coke?"

"Thank you I wouldn't mind, yes I think I'll join you!"

"Don't worry Suzanne, we'll have it here, I'll be back in a minute."

"Thank you darling , you are a star."

(As they   were enjoying their hamburgers, Gloria appeared)

"Good afternoon Gloria how are you today?"

"Not too bad Suzanne, I'm feeling a bit bored, I read yesterday newspaper twice, I can hardly find someone to have a decent conversation!"

"You've got us two, then of course you don't want to be bothered with other people, you are here to relax."

"I cannot relax, I must be doing something all the time that's how I was brought up!"

"Tell you what Gloria maybe you need a good massage, if you want I'll do it for you!"

"That is kind of you Barry, but if I want a massage I know someone who knows how to do it!"

"Let me guess Gloria…"

"You don't need to Suzanne."

"I wish I could find expert who could do that properly, I think my nerves are getting a bit edgy!"

"There you are Barry, you have now a customer, who I'm sure she won't refuse…. Go on then Barry, let me see how you do it."

"As soon as I finish my hamburger Gloria…and you Suzanne you don't mind waiting?"

"Not at all Barry, take your time…."

"Oh I tell you what I was going to ask you Suzanne, you might as well hear this Barry…"

"Thank you Gloria, for a moment I thought it was a secret!"

"Not secret at all. My parents before I left made me an offer, and of course this is all about what I was saying before, like, I must be doing something, they suggested I should open and hairdresser saloon where we live, we own a small property next door which I could use, I told them that I would think about it, and funny enough I was thinking as I was having my breakfast, just about you Suzanne, you could come and run it for me, as I saw you when I came to your hairdresser in Greatstone, I was quite impressed the way you work and treat your customers. What do you think Suzanne?"

"That sounds very interesting Gloria, but you'll have to employ a top hairdresser for that."

"Why? I'm sure you could do that with a couple of apprentices and I'll be helping too, but you would be completely in charge!"

"Thinking about it, I feel whether I have enough experience, I know I am pretty good, as I had quite a few people telling me that…but…"

"But what Suzanne, this could be the chance of your life, and of course it could be my chance to have my own business!"

"First of all I must seriously think about it, and then I must have a chat with my parents, after all I'd like to hear their opinion!"

"Of course darling, you take your time, and nothing's certain yet, but it has been an ongoing idea.!

"What do you think Barry, as you are more or less an entrepreneur!"

"You mean my father is, and very successful too. Yes Suzanne, I think that is a good opportunity for you to upgrade your position.!"

"Thank you Barry, I will make a note of that."

"I must say it was a very interesting afternoon, without the intrusion of that general Manager. If he heard that, which of course he doesn't know it yet, he probably would have wanted the job himself!"

"Be careful Gloria, he probably must be listening, you never know!"

"Thank you girls and thank you for the entertainment, you certainly are not boring you two, I think I will retire now… see you later darlings!"

"Oh… he's getting with it, what did you do to him Suzanne, he's not as shy as I thought!"

"I thought that but I don't think he is, see you later Barry!"

"Must go too Gloria, see you later…."

"Bye, bye Suzanne, don't forget to think seriously about my new venture!"

(The three spent a very interesting afternoon, never thought that Gloria would overcome her boredom, with her new ideas)

Chapter 15

(Eddy and family were having their dinner and Suzanne was telling them about Gloria' s offer about her new venture in her town)

"I think that was nice of her to offer you such chance, after all you have nothing to lose, plus you would be in a better position, to command your wages!"

"Dad is right Suzanne, I think that will be a very nice opportunity for you, now that you have your own car, you wouldn't have any problems to get to Gloria little town!"

"She said she lives in Bloomill. How far is it dad?"

"Only about seven miles, it's very near the sea, apparently they have a very big shopping centre there, we used to go there when you were little."

"I think I slightly remember, but I'm not so sure!"

"You tell her that when we return to England, to let you know exactly what her intentions are, then you can discussed your position!"

"Good… I think I will do that, I have learnt quite a lot in my present job."

"Yes, and I had a lot of your customers commenting on your work, I don't think your employer is that generous, in fact I think he still treats you like a learner, I think three years long enough to be an apprentice!"

"Cor…as usual I made a pig of myself, by eating too much, I think I need a long walk later."

"And a double brandy darling.."

"You said it Claire, are coming with us Suzanne?"

"Yes, I think I might meet our friend Barry, if we are going to the same coffee bar.!

"You seem to like Barry, or am I wrong?"

"He's not bad, he was telling me about his job, he loves brick laying."

"At least he's not a lay about like many others..ah, ah, ah!

"You are right there dad, there are so many around!"

"Who's fault is it? The parents of course, they give everything…in our younger days we didn't get that, because our parent couldn't even afford to pay the bills."

"You are right Claire, you remember I had my first car when I was over twenty eight, and he took me three years to pay for it."

"Oh..here we go…I feel so sorry for you dad."

"So you should sweetheart, money didn't grow on trees then and it still doesn't grow on trees now dear!"

"Don't you start crying now…"

"Just let him say what he wants, but he's right you know?"

"Come on you two, let's go I will treat you to a glass of water tonight…"

"Oh you are sooo funny dad!"

"There they are the Littlewood family…Hello beautiful people!"

"Hello we are waiting for our drinks, tells what you want and I'll go and tell the waiter, so he can bring them all together!"

I start getting a taste of this crème the menthe Laura!"

"I find it quite nice Claire especially if you have eaten too much."

"Hi Barry, Suzanne was telling me that your very good on laying bricks."

"She's exaggerating Eddy, I am alright, and I like doing it, the more I do it the more I learn ways to be faster!"

"Yes Eddy, very soon I won't have to employ brick layers anymore, I shall make him work on his own!"

"You didn't have to go to universsity Barry to learn!"

"Please Eddy don't talk about university, you know something, I think most of the youngsters should learn a proper trade, not ending up reading scholar books."

"Well Fred, Suzanne didn't go to university, as we couldn't afford that then, but she's done well in school and now she's a good hairdresser."

"Good for you Suzanne, I admire you for that, half of Barry's friends are all hanging about waiting to find a job!"

"But don't get me wrong Fred, there are plenty of jobs out there if they want to work, unfortunately some parents they spoil them rotten!"

"Not my boy Eddy, he always had something to do even during school holidays!"

"That's way to do it…..Fred.. Anyway drink up, it's my turn….Same again?"

"Thank you Eddy… I wouldn't say no…."

That's the way Fred, I'm sure we deserve a bit of leisurely life..."

(Meanwhile back at the Hotel John and Gloria were having a quite drink listening to their piano player and telling him about her new venture, with a possible new job for Suzanne)

"You never mentioned anything to me about that Gloria, I wish you could tell more about your life, I am still interested in you...You know?"."

"Sorry darling I think it just went out of my mind. Yes this afternoon I was talking to Suzanne about her job and I told her about my new venture, I got fed up to do that job with that insurance company, and my father suggested to start an hairdresser business, although I haven't got a lot of experience about that kind of trade, nevertheless he suggested that I could employ someone who knows the business, this is why I thought about Suzanne, and for her it'll be a great opportunity!"

"I totally agree with you on that, she's young and very ambitious, I'm sure she could make a success of it!"

"Thank you John, I am so glad that you agree, because that gives me more incentive to do it!"

"By all means, go ahead with it, if you want I can a chat with Suzanne, and suggest she should join you, I was thinking, why don't you offer some kind of partnership."

"Maybe that could would make her more willing to accept my offer...You mean?"

"Yes....In that case you could offer twenty five per cent of shares, and you have the other seventy five, as you put in the property and the set up!"

"I would think that sounds quite fair John..."

"Of course it is, you put the materials and she put the expertise, let me talk to her tomorrow Gloria!"

"Okay John, you have a word with her and see what she says……He surely can play the piano that chap…"

"Yes he does indeed Gloria, he's been here for quite a few months now… shall we make a move now? I've got a nice story to tell you before you fall asleep."
"It better be good, tonight darling, and don't have any ideas, this is just a kind of goodwill for your suggestion!"
"You look very sexy tonight darling, I'm gonna eat you alive… so…..no more complaining in the morning!"
"I will let you know in the morning sexy beast!"
"Mind you Gloria I'm not as virile as I used to be!"
"That happens with your old age… maybe you need some younger stuff, old married men always wish for that, dirty devils!"
"Come off it Gloria, you must admit there a lot of younger girls falling for older men, mind you I don't know what they see in them!"
"That is something I often thought, there must be a reason!"
"Yes darling… here we are…ouch…there's something wrong with this lock, must ask Luigi to have a look at it."

(So the ex marital couple went to their dreams. While Eddy and family was walking back to their hotel, with Suzanne mentioning again to her mum and dad Gloria's interesting offer)

"I have been thinking a lot about that sounds okay to me Suzanne, what do you thing Claire?"

"As I said before it'd be a good opportunity for Suzanne, I don't know Eddy, I think Gloria hasn't any experience on that kind of business, and I wonder if she would exploit Suzanne knowledge for a miserable pay packet!"

"Don't worry mum, maybe Gloria will come up with something good..."

"What would you suggest then mum...maybe offer some money for the set up of the business, and become equal partners!"

"That would be impossible Suzanne, because it would mean risking our savings after all the business is located in a village, which it's not all that big, it would be different if it was in a town centre, then of course I'vet got the garage business coming up, I don't know what Jack's got in his mind."

"I think you have a point there dad, it wouldn't be fair to you... as your job it's quite important more than mine, to involve your money!"

"Thank you Suzanne, I'm glad that you see it that way, then again we have something to tell you that you don't know yet!"

"What is it dad?"

"Well, Jack was telling me just before we left, that he wants to retire, now I don' t know the situation, he told me not to worry about it, but if he's thinking to sell his business to me I doubt very much if I can afford it!"

"Would you be able to rent it from him?"

"That all depends how much the rent would be, however, nothing it's positive yet and these are just talks, let us see what the new day will bring, in the meantime let's enjoy our few last days of holidays!"

"True Eddy, I am quite tired tonight..."

"Maybe you shouldn't have had two crème the menthe!"

"You can shout dad, how many beers did you have?"

"I don't remember, I must have had more than two, I know Fred had quite a few too, and his wife Laura, she a couple of special cocktails, thank goodness you and Barry like coke otherwise I would need a mortgage to take you out!"

"Here we go again mum, Mr. Scrooge has spoken."

"Here we are children, back at our residence!"

"I can your car in the car park dad, look at the lights how they reflect the dirt, perhaps tomorrow you could wash it and get it ready for our departure!"

"Come off of it Suzanne, I'm not going to wash the car over here in the hotel's car park.!

"What's wrong with that? I will help you, it will only take half an hour, if you want I can ask the boy behind the bar if I can have a bucket with some water...! Or maybe with a few Euros he will do it for you."

"Leave off Suzanne, the car is alright as it is, a bit of rain will wash it off...."

"Goodnight…mum, dad… Only joking just wanted to see your reaction dad....See you tomorrow!"

"Good night darling…"

"What an 0065traordinary girl we have there Claire, she really got the gift of the gab...!

Chapter 16

(The sun was shining earlier than usual and Eddy and family were just finishing their breakfast)

"What are you doing today Suzanne, same as usual?"

"Yes mum if you don't mind…. Why don't you and dad come to the swimming pool today, we only have another three days to go?"

"No I think we will stick to our beautiful spot on the beach, don't you think so Eddy?"

"Yes darling as you wish, anything goes for me, first I'll pop over to the paper shop and see if I find yesterday newspaper."

"And I want to get some cream for my sun tan, hoping they have some, yesterday they didn't have any!"

"I'm going mum, see you later you two, I might pop down the beach this afternoon with Barry!"

"Okay darling, and make sure you put some cream on them red patches!"

"I will mum… and don't forget to buy some more, I think I've got very little left!"

"Hello Barry, how do you feel today? And of course it's your last day, looking forward to go home?"

"I think I am Suzanne, I think two weeks in the sun doing nothing it's enough for me, I wouldn't ask for more!"

"Yes …I think the same, after a while it becomes a bit boring, like yourself, I like to do something!"

"When are you leaving then Suzanne?"

"We have another three days, including today, I expect I will see you early next week!"

"Well, you have my phone number and email address, contact me as soon as you get home!"

"I will Barry, you can count on that, I think I'm going to miss you, coming down here and not seeing you!"

"Do you really mean that Suzanne?"

"Of course I do, otherwise I wouldn't say it…I do like you, you know?"

"In which way Suzanne, as a friend or….?"

"Well… Barry let me put it this way, at home I'm sure we shall get better acquainted with each other, time will tell!"

"But I want you to know that I like you very much, if anything I'm just about to fall in love with you, please give me a little bit of incentive."

"Don't be silly Barry, you don't need incentive to fall in love, love just come natural, this is why there's a saying; love at first sight!"

"I know that Suzanne, but how can I love you, when I feel that you don't."

"Maybe your feelings or shall I say your love for me, is call platonic love."

"Excuse my ignorance but what's the meaning of platonic love?"

"Well, as far as I know platonic love, is that kind of love that is no sexual business nor romantic!"

"Something like brother and sister?"

"Not really, that is a different love, I would think you could say familiar love, or brotherly love."

"But…but..Suzanne I like you very, very much, and I can tell you...That's how I felt when first I saw you!"

"What did you feel when first you saw me then?"

" I felt somehow, inside me a feeling, that I thought; She' s so beautiful….Yes I could fall in love with a girl like that, but a few times, you tried to put me off, probably because I am not your type and I do understand that..Is it possible?"

"Yes that could be possible too, but when you say that you are not my type, I think you are wrong, don't forget that love grow with time like anything else!"

(So involve in their conversation they didn't even see Gloria coming)

"Hello you too, goodness me your conversation must be so important, that you made me feel ignored!"

"Oh hello Gloria, you look very springy and sprung this morning, I guess you slept well last night!"

"How did you guess Suzanne? I really slept eight hours, very unusual for me, as I am a very poor sleeper, of course I want to make the best of it, because tomorrow afternoon I shall leave in peace, actually today you just look like two love birds!"

"Thank you Gloria, we were just talking about how many ways a man or a woman could fall in love!"

"That's right Barry, when John and I met, neither of us would have thought that we could fall in love with each other!"

"Is that so Gloria? In that case you have just given me some hope, with a girl, who I might fall in love!"

"Oh Barry.. Barry…? Let me guess…"

"Please Gloria don't say another word, you could make me feel embarrassed!"

"I think we better change subject, shall we talk about you Gloria..?come on then give us some lecture of your past."

"Why not Suzanne, forget the past.... in fact I've got some present news for you, last night I was telling John about that possible idea I mentioned yesterday, and I think he came with a very easy solution, which I'm sure you'll like it...He'll probably will tell you that himself..."

"I shall look forward to hear that, he does come up with some good ideas now and then.!"

"Right, I fancy a nice campari before my lunch, how about you Susanne!"

"Nothing strong, perhaps an unalcoholic drink, they got plenty here in Italy…"

"I'll have one thank you…"

"Well Barry, since you are the only man in the party, I suggest you go and get them…"

"It will be my pleasure dear ladies!"

(While Barry went to get the drinks, Gloria took the liberty to ask Suzanne a few personal questions)

"Now then Suzanne, what do you think of Barry then?"

"I don' t know Gloria, for some unknown reasons, there is something which I cannot see very clearly, he's a nice boy, he says he loves me, or let me say; he likes me!"

"Maybe he does Suzanne, you must give him a chance."

"I think he likes my body a lot, he's not very conversational, I like someone who I can talk to, maybe with the time he will improve!"

"You certainly seem to be more mature than him, funny I never thought about John when I met him to be below my standards!"

"John is a clever man if I may say so Gloria, he's got the gift of the gab, and he knows how to talk to people!"

"But let me say something about Barry, before he gets here, he told me the other night that, he really thinks the world of you, if anything, he said that he could fall in love with you very easy!"

"That is nice to hear Gloria, thank you, maybe my thoughts toward him could be wrong!"

"Yes they could be, I would hate to see you ending up with a better looking fellow but a lazy bastard!"

"I like your summing up Gloria…."

"Here we are ladies, your favourites drinks, with a lot of ice, and I asked the barman for some olives and little bits, just look what he's done for two beautiful ladies!"

"Listen to him Suzanne, sounds like he's the perfect entertainer."

"I can do even better my dear ladies!"

"I am impressed Barry, I think you deserve ten out of ten!"

"Thank you gorgeous Suzanne for your compliment!"

"Hello, hello…two beautiful ladies with just one man? I wish that would happen to me now and then!"

"I can see that you are jealous uncle John, why don't you get yourself a drink and join us!"

"I thought you can treat me to a drink, mean lot!"

"Treat you, it's like giving water to the sea, you have everything you want!"

"Thank you Gloria, I was only joking, anyway, I haven't got a lot of time for you all, as my big bosses are about to appear for the usual weekly meeting!"

"You busy bee… we'll see you this afternoon then."

"No doubt you will, and bytheway Suzanne, I would like to have a little chat with you later!"

"Of course uncle, anytime!"

"I'll see you at the open restaurant John for a bite to eat, don't forget that today is my last day for you to put up with me!"

"Of course sweetheart, don't I know that, see you later, I think in an hour!"

(His meeting didn't take long and by lunch time John was free to join Gloria for a bite to eat down at the open restaurant)

"Ah this is lovely, you know Gloria, I really do enjoy my job here in Italy, of course the only problem is that you are not here with me!"

"You lying so and so….I don't think you mean that!"

"Come on Gloria, how many times do I have to tell you that I do regret our divorce, and I'm sure you do too!"

"Perhaps I do John, at home in England there are days when I really miss you!"

"More than once I did offer you to come down here, but you always turned me down!"

"I think I listened to my parents a little bit too much!"

"I know that Gloria, it's about time that you make your own decisions, and of course there was no need for you to divorce me for that little escapade."

"Mind you that was the only one I knew, I wonder how many you have had!"

"Now..now Gloria you are exaggerating a bit!"

"No I am not, my mother was right, she thought the world of you, but since you done that, you put her off!"

"No matter what your mother thinks of me, she's a lovely person!"

"She knows that you like her, because before I left, she said to me; try to be nice to John…I still think he's a lovely man!"

"Thank you for telling me this, and now eat your lunch and let us stop bickering, later I've got to go back to the office, I've got a pile of correspondence to sort out!"

(After lunch Gloria joined Suzanne and Barry, and they were still having their usual hamburger)

"Had a nice lunch Gloria?"

"Not too bad Suzanne, started off with the usual bickering but ended with a magical kiss!"

"You two just sound like my parents Gloria, first arguing and then lovey - dovey!"

"That' what I call a perfect union Barry!"

"I expect you'll have a romantic dinner tonight Gloria, being your last day on the Riviera!"

"I expect nothing extra ordinary, since he's more attached to his job than to his ex wife!"

"I tell you what you should do you two, perhaps you should join our table, I find my dinners so boring with my parents, at least I shall have someone to talk to."

"that's a good idea Barry, I think we should invite Suzanne and her parents too, I'm sure my John will be able to afford three extra dinners, I think I'm going to ask him later, what do you think Suzanne…"**(shouting to her thinking she was half asleep)**

"I heard that Gloria, it's okay by me, if my uncle wants to invite us, that will make a change from our hotel!"

"Right I'm going to look for John then , and I will let you know very soon!"

"There she goes, look at her Barry, she looks like a general, I bet she don't ask him, but tell him!"

"Ah, ah, ah, ah, I wouldn't be surprise Suzanne!"

"You know what I really think Barry….Gloria is the right woman to my uncle in line, pity they are divorced."

"But you never know... Suzanne they'll probably get together again sometime sooner than you think!"

"You are probably right Barry!"

"I really hope so.... although I am not so sure!"

"What makes you think that Suzanne?"

"I just got that intuition, let us say a woman one!"

"You are some girl....You know?"

"Thank you Barry...and you some boy...!"

Chapter 17

(It didn't take long for Gloria to convince John for the get together... Twenty minutes later she was is back with her answer, and very pleased about it)

"No problem Barry, okay Suzanne? Tonight he will arrange a table for eight at seven thirty, he said he'll be more than pleased to host us all!"

"That's wonderful Gloria thank you very much, don't know what we would do without you..... you are a star!"

"Oh...bytheway, he's in his office, when you have five minutes, he said if you could pop in, he wants to have a word with you!"

"Actually, I need to go to the ladies, I'll go now!"

"I bet you are dying to hear what he's got to say!"

"Too right I am, and you Barry don't laugh, this is not a laughing matter!"

"Typical nosey woman...sorry.. I don't really mean that, good luck darling!"

"I know you don't mean it.... my love, see you in a jiffy!"

"Oh...my love eh? Things are getting better!"

(It didn't take long for Suzanne to get to John's office, actually she thought to see him before going to the ladies)

(Knock, knock…) "Come in whoever you are…"

"It's only me uncle, did you want to see me?"

"Yes my darling, so let's get down to the nitty-gritty, take a seat Suzanne and listen carefully; I suppose you know about Gloria's new venture, of course you know, what am I saying? Well, I came up with the idea that if she wants to open and hairdresser saloon without any knowledge about the business, she may well do so, but if she employ you, which you know the business pretty well, I suggested that she should finance it completely plus give you a twenty five per cent stake or shares of the profits, call it what you like, plus of course a monthly wage, to be agreed by both parties!"

"That sounds very fair uncle, which it means that she would get seventy five and twenty five for me, but how long that would be for such arrangement?"

"She hasn't mentioned that, but if the business is successful, every year she should increase your shares by some per cent, not exceeding forty per cent, and of course you wouldn't own the premises and the contents. How's that sound to you then?"

"Sounds fine, but I like to have a word with my parents first, that is before I agree!"

"Of course my dear, I tell you what'll do; I will write down all this and give you a copy each, as tomorrow Gloria is leaving, so you know where you both stand.

"Do you think she will agree? I'm quite surprise that she rely on your suggestions, mind I think they are quite fair."

"Thank you for your opinion... I'm sure she will darling, I will give a copy before you go back to your hotel, so you'll be able to show it to your dad and mum."

"Uncle have you got any more of that cream?"

"Yes I have but I think you'll have to ask your Barry to put it on, I don't want a surprise visit from Gloria while I do that."

"Oh.. you are so suspicious uncle, I wasn't even thinking about...what you thought."

"As if I didn't know you... you are tremendously clever my dear niece!"

(In that moment a couple knocks on the door)

"Come in..... Oh... it's you Gloria, we were just talking about you, I explained my idea to Suzanne, which I will write down forthwith and give you both a copy, I shall keep one... just in case of a dispute!"

"That's fine with me John, I shall look forward to read that, and naturally I'll have to show it to my parents too! What's your opinion Suzanne?"

"As far as I'm concerned I think it's a fair agreement, I like it very much, and if this materializes I can promise you that you won't be sorry... not with the amount of regulars that I already have!"

"That is very reassuring Suzanne, I'm quite confident we will both succeed."

"I am sure you both will, you are very responsible and hungry for success."

"Thank you John, I shall go back and have a nice soak in the bath...See you both at dinner then."

"See you later darling."

(Gloria leaves the office)

"I cannot believe how lucky we are, see? I told you that she would come around, and supposing you'd made one of yours funny moves, we would have been really in trouble,"
"Yes you are right, but I'm a bit upset when I think what you done last night...You sexy uncle..."
"I've done what I had to do darling, it was more or less a duty...that's all....Here's your cream and go back to Barry, I'm sure he'll enjoy doing that!"
"I don't think I will...Your hands are better!"

(Barry did the right job with the cream, and in return she put some on him, and they both went off to sleep, until an hour later John woke them up and gave an envelope to Suzanne)
"This for you, just let my brother and your mum to read and see what they'll say."
"Thank you uncle... I think I shall go now and we'll see you at dinner...Oh is it at the main restaurant or down here in the open?"
"It is in the main restaurant, we'll meet at seven in the bar, okay you two?"
"Thank you.... no problems!"

(Back at the Sea View Hotel Suzanne told her parents about the dinner at the Hotel Riviera, which they were delighted to accept and told too once again about Gloria's new venture, and show them what John had written down, which was exactly what he suggested, but it looked like some kind of agreement. Eddy and Claire read it very carefully and they seemed to agree, naturally knowing that didn't have to put any of their money toward it)

"I like it Suzanne, I think it's very fair, what do you think Claire?"

"Yes I agree, considering that Gloria might not do as much work as you Suzanne, but on second thoughts, I'm sure she's always be there to do something!"

"You have a point there Claire, there again we'll see what happens."

"I think personally the offer it's quite good, further more if we are successful my shares will go up gradually!"

"Yes darling I think we both agree, let us wait and see what will happen with Gloria's parents!"

(They all met at the Riviera bar for some drinks and then they sat down to a lovely dinner with the coffee and liqueurs out on the terrace overlooking the sea)

"That was a superb dinner John, thank you very much, no need to tell you how much Claire and I and Suzanne we fully appreciate...you have been helpful and most kind!"

"Please brother don't even mention it, that's the least I can do....You know something Fred, my brother never ask me for anything, he always wants to depend from his own pocket!"

I understand what you mean John, probably I would be the same as your brother if I had a brother like you!"

"Thank you Fred, and bytheway, you didn't' t have to buy those two bottles of wine, however, thank you very much, it was a super vintage!"

My pleasure, John, my pleasure!"

"Mum can I have a little walk around the gardens with Barry."

"Of course my dear, don't' be too long it's already ten thirty, I can see your father closing his eyes!"

"That's typical your mum darling when she wants to go to bed."

"Don't take any notice of her dad, she's only worried about her beauty sleep!"

"See what that mean Gloria… that is what happen in a family, and I simply love it, pity I never had the chance of experiencing it!"

"You are still in time John, just give up your second celibacy, thigh the knot once again and get cracking on the production!"

"Thank you Fred, I shall give it a thought, in the meantime, I better go to the reception and see if everything is alright."

"Don't be too long John I've ordered another brandy for you!"

"At this rate he won't even find his own bed tonight, and don't forget that he must take me to the airport tomorrow morning!"

"I'm sure he'll be alright in the morning, he's a strong boy!"

(the evening ended wonderfully and everyone went to their own way, Claire had to go and find Suzanne who was sitting near the pool with Barry, and surprising finding them having a snuggling session, Mum Claire made some funny noises trying to avoid embarrassment for them and Barry jump up from his deck chair all scared….."

"Hello Mrs. Collins, just didn't see you coming, we are ready to come back too!"

"For goodness sake Barry, don't worry, she won't bite you."

"No, I won't Suzanne, but I think we should go back to our hotel now…….it's nearly midnight"

"Oh, alright mum...I'm coming...See you tomorrow Barry!"

"We must say bye, bye to Gloria, as she's leaving early tomorrow morning...I'm going back to see her now..."
"Okay mum...we are coming with you."
"Hi Gloria, it has been a wonderful evening.. shame you are going tomorrow, but in a couple days we shall leave too!"
"Yes, for me not only it has been a nice evening but also a very nice week, which brought back some memories, It was nice to see you both again after such a long time, and I hope we can do something about that new venture of mine, I am really looking forward to do it!"
"Yes, Eddy and I are very pleased that you offered Suzanne such a big chance to show her capabilities in her profession!"
"I did it because I saw what she can do, don't you Suzanne?"
"Well, I will try my best Gloria, as I said I won't let you down."
"However, when you all return to England please give me a call, as we must meet again to discuss other things!"
"Of course we will Gloria, in the meantime you have a nice journey tomorrow, and you John, try to get her safe at the airport, not stopping in the way....ah, ah, ah, ah!"
"No chance of that Claire... Thank you all for your company. Goodnight all....
"And good night to you both....Goodnight Fred, Laura, and all of you.....!"

Chapter 18

(Early next day John and Gloria were on their way to the airport, this time he took the motorway, so he made much quicker, as they were quite early for her flight, they thought to have a coffee in the passengers lounge)

"It was nice to see you again John, I really enjoyed my week with you, you know, sometimes I think we shouldn't have split up and divorced so fast."

"Well.. first of all I am so glad that you came to Italy, and I am so pleased that you enjoyed your vacation, the other thing is… Yes, I think we should have never divorced, I really didn't want that to happen, but it must have been faith!"

"Talk about faith, that's a joke, it was me really, of course if I haven't met Vicky in the first place, nothing would have happened, perhaps thinking rightly it was faith!"

"Never mind eh? Look John let us both think about it, and the future might bring us together again!"

"I hope so, although, I have now sampled life as an independent, I wonder if I will get used to married life again."

"That's not very reassuring John, so, does it mean that if I am hoping for a future reunion, I don't really stand a chance?"

"Don't be silly darling, I was just supposing after all, we haven't been together for nearly five years!"

"I suppose you are right John…When do you think I will see you then?"

"In a couple of months I'll be having my yearly holidays, so I'll be able to come and see you, for two or three weeks, and I'm sure we shall probably take it from there, in fact if you decide to do that new venture of yours, I'll probably, be there to give you an helping hand!"

"That would nice John. Yes I think I will do that new venture, you see…I've got to do something, I can't sit in front of that desk all day long!"

"I know you are not the type to do waste your time like that….I think they are calling your flight darling…"

"Yes you are right, I think I better go….Bye, bye darling, please do come soon…"

"Do I see a few tears rolling down your face…? Come cheer up, it's not the end of the world.!"

"True John, I shall ring you as soon as I get home…."

(A fond embrace and the two went different ways)

(During his journey back, John was seriously thinking to start a new life with Gloria, although, he probably would miss his independent life in the sunshine, never the less he would gain a quite married life, after all she was the only daughter and the parents were quite well off. He thought that wasn't right to think things like that, but it was a fact, and not a dream, and so he arrived back at the Hotel Riviera)

"Hello uncle, Gloria went off alright then?"

"Yes darling and she sends her regards too, and she told me to tell you not to forget the new venture., because she really looking forward to do it!"

"I've been thinking nearly all night long, I think I am quite excited about it, and my parents are too, of course I will miss you tremendously, not seeing you around there, after you are my favourite only uncle!"

"Nice of you to say that, in fact Gloria and I have been talking of getting together again, of course that's not final, but there's that chance!"

"That'll be nice uncle, a bit disappointed in my heart, but I suppose I'll get used to it, further more I'll be near you, as the new business will be under your roof!"

"Watch what you saying darling....I see Barry coming along....Hello Barry.. I see you are all geared up for your morning swim!"

"Yes John I've got to make the best of it as today is our last one, are you pleased to get rid of us!"

"Nonsense Barry, we will miss your money, as you are a paying costumer."

"I'm only joking, I certainly will miss you and your good food, and of course the swimming pool."

"Why don't you ask your father to do one, I'm sure you have enough land where you live!"

"Yes we got plenty land, but my father said more than once, a swimming pool is a waste of money in England, as we haven't got the sunshine you have here!"

"I suppose your father is right, but there's always another option, which you can have one undercover."

"Ah....That's not the same John, what do you think Suzanne?"

"Well... I think if I would marry someone with a bit of money, I certainly would like a covered swimming pool in my house!"

"There you are Barry, you might have a covered swimming pool then when you get married!

"I don't know so much John, maybe that particular bride will not want one, if she can't swim!"

"But Barry.....I can swim...."

"Ah, ah, ah ah...I can see you are blushing Barry...Did you really mean that Suzanne?"

"I'm not going to answer that in front of you uncle, as it doesn't concern you...ah, ah, ah, ah!"

"I'm sorry I spoke young lady, just in case I hope I shall be invited.."

"I think I can hear your phone ringing uncle...."

"That's true...I think I'd better be going, see you later beautiful people!"

"Your uncle is quite a boy Suzanne, he certainly knows the facts of life..."

"Yes, he certainly knows what he's doing Barry, I find him quite clever, I mean, came to Italy without a job, worked as a washer up in a restaurant, becomes a waiter, then assistant manager and now general manager of this five star hotel, which is one of the biggest on the Riviera, I'd say, not a bad run up the ladder in almost five years!"

"Well, I am very impressed Suzanne, I guess there aren't many around like him!"

"Oh I forgot...when he did marry Gloria he was penniless, and wham.... there he was in the money."

"Silly boy then leaving his beautiful situation for another woman then..."

"Yes that was a silly mistake, which he's still regrets, but Gloria still loves him, I reckon she'll have him back anytime, if wishes to do so!"

"Must admit, he's a lucky man then."

"Mind you if a husband of mine would go to bed with another woman, I don't think I would have him back, I can tell you that, and for goodness sake Barry, keep this conversation to yourself, don't even tell your parents!"

"I promise you that, don't worry, these matters are very delicate, to the person involved!"

"Shall we have a swim Suzanne? Then I shall go and get the usual hamburger!"

"I'm a bit fed up of hamburgers, is there anything else?"

"Why don't you come with me, there's a big variety of food there including drinks!"

(They have swim and then a very enjoyable lunch snack, followed by a snooze, being woken up by Barry's mother)

"Come on you lazy bagger, I think you better go and do your suitcase, in the morning you won't have time, as the coach to the airport will leave early!"

"Sorry mum, I will come up in ten minutes, let me wake up properly...."

"Alright Barry, I think I'll go up now and get your dad clothes from the laundry!"

"Will I see you at the coffee bar tonight Suzanne!"

"I don't really know what my parents will do, I will try, anyway we already exchange phone numbers and emails, so I will get in touch myself as soon as I get home!"

"You won't let me down Suzanne....please? You know how I feel about you, although, I did not show my feeling s to you as you might expected!"

"I am surprise that you realized that Barry, I think I like the way you expressed yourself right now!"

"Suzanne just in case I won't see you again before I leave... **(And very gently they kissed each other with a very warm and sensuous meaning of love)**

"God that was nice Barry, might see you tonight, please go, you don't want to upset your mum!"

"Bye, bye darling .....I love....you, **(blowing another kiss Suzanne did likewise with a smile)**

(Whilst not too distant she noticed her uncle talking to Luigi the porter as he was piling up the lounge bed-chairs, Suzanne waved at her uncle as he was approaching her)

"I see your lover boy has left you already, joking darling!"

"I know you are uncle... his mum called him to go and do his suitcase, and get ready for tomorrow's early departure!"

"Oh yes tomorrow they are leaving, what a nice family, don't you think so Suzanne?"

"Yes they are Uncle, and he is a nice boy, you know he just told me that he loves me!"

"Nothing wrong in that Suzanne, I'm so pleased for you!"

"I am not so sure how how much I feel for him..."

"Given time and you will see that everything will work out for the best!"

"It's easy for you to say....bytheway, have you got anymore of that cream in your office?"

"Not really but I have some in my chalet, I'll go and get it!"

"Can I come uncle, I am rather curious to see your accommodation...."

"Well... I shouldn't really, I wouldn't want anyone to see us going in and giving some food for thoughts!"

"Sometimes you are so suspicious.. come on...Please?"

"Oh... okay but promise me you'll behave yourself!"

"I will don't worry....

(And so they went both to his chalet, John went to the bathroom to get the cream, and she followed him, while he was looking in the cupboard, she put her arms around his waist very tight, he turned around and look at each other without saying a word....and he said;)

"Please Suzanne don't do this it's not right"

"Please uncle don't turn me down, if you do, I will hate you so much, you've got to shut down this fire inside me!"

"Suzanne you know that we shouldn't do this....Please!!"

(She took him by his hand to his bed and they both fell into that fire making her cry with pleasure....but John felt so guilty as if he had committed a murder)

"Please forgive me darling, you dam well knew I didn't want this to happen, for Christ sake I am your uncle!"

"Don't be sorry uncle I should be the guilty one, but no one is hurt... I am happy now, that you extinguished that fire, which has been burning for a long time, let us say that it never happened, and let us promise, that we shall keep this secret in our hearts forever..... where is that cream I need it, just put it on very gently...ooh...uncle thank you!"

"That's it darling, and please let me go out first and see if anyone's about.......come on.... out quick....!"

(Suzanne went back to the pool as if nothing had happened and started to spread her cream on the front of her body too, thinking about his gentle touch and smiling to herself)

Chapter 19

(Suzanne and family were having dinner at their hotel, and they were contemplating what to do on their last day)

"Barry was so sad today thinking he was leaving us behind, quite a nice boy….You know?"

"Yes Suzanne, I think he is a nice boy, he seems very clean, and of course is very well educated."

"What do you mean clean mum?"

"Well I mean he has no tattoos on his body, today it seems to me that those are the fashion, how can some ruin their beautiful bodies?"

"Yes it's true that mum, I don't particular like tattoos myself, but if someone wants to have them… let them, it's their own body and not mine! And yes, that's true he's very polite indeed, and you know something I think he's in love with me, mind you he hasn't said much these days, I think he's a bit shy, and afraid to be turned down!"

"Well girl, if he likes you he'll probably will say it sooner or later, I wouldn't rush things!"

"Thanks dad your opinion is very valuable!"

"Anyway, we are nearly at the end of our holiday, did you enjoy it Suzanne?"

"Oh yes…I did indeed…thank you for giving me that!"

"It was our pleasure too darling, we did enjoy as much as you I guess, in fact the arrangement of you at the swimming pool and us down at the beach, it just the ideal choice!"

"That's very true dad, at least you had some time to yourselves, to talk about things that you don't usually talk at home, and what are we going to do tomorrow, as it is our last day? Perhaps I was thinking to come down to the beach with you young people!"

"Enough of this young people, otherwise I shall put you in a care home with the old people when we go back home!"

"If you decide to do that dad, please make sure to put me in a care home with men only, I don't particularly like to look after old women!"

"You'll be an old woman yourself one day, don't worry about that!"

"Oh… you are a lovely dad… and I love you lot and of course you too mum…"

"Thank you darling…Oh I know….You are dad's girl!"

"Thank you mum, you are both the same to me, and thank you for making me a true female girl!"

"Eddy I think we ought to go to the usual coffee bar tonight, as we haven't said goodbye to the Tenders!"

"Yes… I think Barry said they might go there tonight!"

"Okay I'll finish my pudding and then we'll go!"

(The bar was as usual full but they managed to get a table outside, so they could se if Barry's family was coming along, and naturally talk of the devil..... there they were walking along)

"Hello Fred… come on then we kept a chairs for you!"

"Thanks Eddy, very kind of you, we were saying that we didn't want to leave you here without saying goodbye!"
"We said the same thing Fred, actually it was our Suzanne to suggest it, now then what would you like?"
"No Eddy let me get these…!"
"Look here Fred you bought us the very first drink in this bar, so now let me get the last for you lot!"
"Alright if you insist Eddy…."

(And so another evening in a good company, and making plans to meet each other back in England)

"You must come to our place for dinner Fred and Laura, and naturally you too Barry!"
"We'll be delighted, then of course you can come and visit us, as I want you to try my culinary expertise, I love cooking…You know?"
"You know something Claire, Fred won't let me in that kitchen when he's cooking, he's absolutely terrible…"
"Mind you Claire when she says terrible she's not talking about my cooking , she's talking about my temper!"
"I presume just like all chefs, they are all temperamental!"
"I often thought that is the heath of the stove that makes them like that Laura."
(And looking at Barry and Suzanne)
"I thought that too Claire, look at them two they are whispering I don't know what…"
"Go on let them whisper Laura, they don't want to know our silly old discussions…mind you what else can we talk about? So many years went by and now we have reached the point when I think we probably run out of subjects!"

"You probably run out of subjects dear Fred, and you rarely keep awake at home after dinner!"

"Don't worry Laura, Eddy is the same, he has to have a couple of glasses of wine and a little brandy, and off he goes!"

"Sounds like we are home already Fred...never mind, that's life, it was a great pleasure to meet you, and thanks to my brother John!"

"Your brother Eddy... he surely is a boy, he'll never die of starvation, he really has his own personality, but that's what you want when you are dealing with costumers in catering business!"

"You are right Fred, he has good personality, and really knows how to talk to people!"

"True, pity he broke up with Gloria, she's not a bad girl, actually.....he's had it made there, her family is quite well off, and she's the only daughter!"

"Dad, money is not everything in life, if he wasn't happy, what's the use?"

"Come off it Suzanne, he didn't have to shake up with another girl, Gloria is a beautiful girl."

"Don't we know it....!!

"You be quiet Fred, you don't know the ins and outs!"

"Sorry darling, just paying a compliment how nice Gloria is, after all I'm entitle of my opinion!"

"Actually it was the other women that was after John!"

"How do you know that Suzanne?"

"Gloria told me, yes mum, she told yesterday when we were sitting around the pool!"

"See what I mean? We never know the real story until is told by the writer!"

"What do you mean by that mum?"

"Just a saying darling….Just a saying!"
"Well Eddy, Claire and Suzanne, I think we better call it a day, we have a long day tomorrow, not so much the flight, but the waiting at check in passports, and so on and then before that we might even come across some traffic jam!"

(They all say goodbye to each other with a few kisses, and off they went to their own hotels)

"Lovely people them Tenders, yes, very pleasant and good company, we must have them over for dinner in the next few weeks!"
"If you say so Eddy, I think he's alright, she seems a little bit stuck up, maybe she thinks we are not the same level as them. You know what I mean Eddy?"
"I don't know Claire, maybe you are right, but sometime we can be wrong."
"And you Suzanne what's your honest opinion?"
"I don't know mum, I don't think you can criticize a person in a few days, I must admit I thought Barry was different than I thought, but in the last few days, he turned out to be himself, what he's really like, I think he's quite nice!"
"I found him a bit quiet, now you've got to be careful of the quiet ones!"
"No mum, I think he's just plain, he mean what he says, not like some others, when they talk they are full of bullshit.."
"Mind your language girl, good job there's nobody about!"
"Nothing wrong by saying that Claire, for goodness sake, you are not a nun are you!"
"Ah, ah, ah, ah I like that dad, you tell her…!"
"I always thought you two are an apple split in two!"
"What do you mean by that Claire?"

"Never mind darling...Goodnight Suzanne...see you at breakfast..."
"Goodnight mum, goodnight dad!"

(Next day the Collins are down at breakfast earlier than usual)

"Good lord Claire they have some bacon this morning, mind you it's not the same as ours, still, I think I'm going to have some...."
"Dad that is not bacon, that is Parma ham, it looks like bacon, but it tastes differently, the Italians eat it with melon or they have as a starter with some salami, before their main meals!"
"Looks like bacon to me, mind you is cut very thinly, just don't know how they could cut it like that!"
"Dad they have a machine called slicer, see what I mean, in England in certain things we are behind times!"
"I think it's a bit salty, I still prefer our bacon!"
"You'll have plenty of that in England Eddy, please stop moaning, you sound like an eighty year old man!"
"I think I should get a medal for putting up with you two!"
"If you should get a medal, what do you think I should get darling for looking after you!"
"Listen to your mum Suzanne, she thinks I couldn't cope on my own!"
"Maybe she's right dad, I've never seen you doing the cooking, cleaning the house, doing the ironing and many other things!"
"Alright, alright..you win, but don't expect me to do all those things when we get home, I have enough on my plate at Jack's garage. That's another problem to solve!"

"Now don't start worrying about Jack Eddy, you'll do that when you'll start work, I'm sure Jack won't let you be without a job, if anything he might have already worked out what to do, knowing him he's a good and fair man!"

"Right lets go and get ready then, we'll go down to the beach…Claire go and get the staff ready!"

"See what we mean dad, it would be nice if, I mean if just for once you would get things ready and not ask mum!"

"That's no problem my dear, just tell me where to find everything we need!"

"Never mind softy, drink up your coffee and come up stairs……

Chapter 20

(Meanwhile back at the Hotel Riviera, John was saying goodbye to the Tenders)

"You have a nice journey Fred, and with a bit of luck I shall see you all in a few months!"
"Don't worry John I'm sure we'll see you back in Bloom Mill with Gloria…"
"I might just do that Fred…"
"Bye, bye to you all…."

(John was soon back at the reception, and by pure chance there was Ispettore Lancini talking to Jean the receptionist)

"Good morning Ispettore, nice to see you, what's the problem then?"
"Actually can I have a word with you in private!"
"Of course Ispettore, please come to my office, can I offer you a coffee or maybe a real cup of English tea, that's one the things I am not short of!"
"No thank you…I just had a coffee before I arrived here…..it is a very quick visit!"

"So please tell me....What can I do for you Ispettore, I hope it's nothing bad, but there again now days with all these nasty people about, you can expect anything!"

"Well, the lawyer of your predecessor or shall I say Signor Luca Vanni, has contacted me and of course Signor Vanni is not very happy about his innocence, so his lawyer decided to make some more enquiries by asking us to supply them your finger prints, I am sorry but you'll have to come to our station where they will take your finger prints there, unfortunately we have no choice."

"This is rather annoying Ispettore, and I would think a waste of my precious time."

"Well...I must warn you that if you decline, you might be even arrested for not comply with the Italian law!"

"But Ispettore..if the case was closed, is it normal to reopen it?"

"Certainly Mr. Collins, it is the rights of the citizen, no matter which country you are from."

"Okay then..I'll be down at your station sometime this afternoon...hold on a second, I just remember that I have something important today, how about tomorrow afternoon?"

"That will be just fine Mr. Collins.. say about three pm?"

"Fine, tomorrow afternoon...tell me how long will it take for the results?"

"Well..probably one week or ten days, because we have to send them your finger prints, they have to examine them plus the magistrate have the final saying, but don't worry everything will be alright!"

"On the other hand Ispettore..it is rather a nuisance as for a little mistake on their side it could ruin my name."

"I don't understand what you mean Mr. Collins, I don't think there will be any mistakes, finger prints are like some kind of DNA - so there cannot be any complications."

"Well... I just thought perhaps there was a way of avoiding all this unfortunate business.!

"I don't see any other solutions, all I can say is I'm very sorry to drag you in again.!

"I can assume that Mr. Vanni is still very upset by losing his job, and certainly not very happy in his new one!"

"That's what I thought Mr. Collins, anyway I expect to see you tomorrow and please make sure you'll be there, bye!"

"Bye, bye Ispettore...see you tomorrow!"

(John waited for the Inspector to leave, and then he sat down and whispered to himself;) " Bloody hell I think I need a double brandy, I just didn't want this to happen, not when everything seemed to be okay with my situation..."
(And so he poured himself a large brandy, which he kept in his cupboard behind his desk)

(Meanwhile Suzanne and family were down on the beach having good fun)

"I say Claire shall we have some lunch, down there on that kiosk over there later on?"

"Why not darling, I noticed yesterday it was completely full, their food must be good!"

"That's the kind of places you must try when you go on holidays, the more expensive they are, the worst they get."

"Actually remember when we went to Spain last time, and we used to go in those back street little places, they really were very good value for money!"

"That's true mum, the girl I work with she told me the same thing, she went to Greece and they used to do just that!"

(Later there they were trying the little place in question)

"What a lovely place this is Claire, look we are only a few yards from the water, you can smell the fish!"

"Yes Eddy…I think I shall miss this beach, I wouldn't mind to come back here again!"

"That shouldn't be any problem, in actual fact I was speaking to the owner of our hotel, blamey he does speaks good English the fellow, he said he learned it in London when he was working as a waiter for a couple of years.

"Is that where he learned his English? I was wondering, how he picked it up so well!"

"Anyway, he was saying that if we ever decide to come back, he said to give him a call six months before and we can book it without deposit, he said; you come and you pay when you leave, you wouldn't get that in our Country!"

"For sure you wouldn't…..I can tell you that!"

"Here Suzanne.. Any ideas how much John's hotel charges per week?"

"Yes… I picked up one of their brochures and he said for a double room for two people is just over two thousand pounds if you want all inclusive you have to add another five hundred!"

"So it means the Tenders' bill must have been nearly five grand!"

"Not far from that dad…"

"Bloody hell, I reckon our is just over fifteen hundred, plus of course the travelling!"

"They also had to pay for extra travelling...." "Quite a packet ....still they can afford it..."

"That's it another good lunch, I think I've got an idea Claire, for my usual packed lunch, I'll expect you to me something like this, I don't really care anymore for a couple of spam sandwiches and a banana during my break, even Jack has a better lunch than me!"

"Then you better have lunch with Jack my dear Eddy, or if you want a better lunch you'll have to increase my weekly housekeeping money!"

"Here we go again, I think you two will end up in a divorce at this rate, and that it cost me more money to come and visit you, where ever you will be!"

"Goodness me Suzanne, your imagination has no end, let me tell you my dear, that by the time we divorce we'll be both in a care home!"

"That I won't allow it mum, no matter how many children I'll have, I'll still be able to look after you and dad...provide my future husband will help too!"

(The glorious afternoon was nearly over, and the time arrived to pack up and go back to the hotel, and pack up the suitcases for an early departure to old England, but before doing that they thought to pop in at the Riviera to say bye, bye to John, but unfortunately he wasn't there, Eddy told the receptionist the they will pop in the morning)

"I have checked the car Claire, and although I haven't used fit for a couple of weeks, it started strait away!"

"One thing I must say, being married to a car mechanic, is quite useful, and I love you for that."

"Thank you darling, nice to get a good compliment for a change!"

"She's not too bad dad, it's you the moaner, more than anything!"

"I think we better go downstairs for our last dinner!"

"Too right dad…I'm hungry tonight!"

(Dinner was as usual very pleasant, and so was the coffee, the owner presented Claire and Suzanne a little scarf, local homemade and for Eddy he gave him a couple bottles of red wine and a bottle of Amaretto liqueur)

"Thank you Giovanni, I don't think we'd expected this, it's very kind of you!"

"It us we have to thank you Mr. Collins for using our hotel."

"Never the less, we thank you Giovanni for your kind thought!"

"Nothing could give me more pleasure than this, you have been a very pleasant family, and we appreciate your custom, hope you will come back again!"

"Well Giovanni, I think I better settle now so in the morning we won't waste time as we have quite a long way to go."

"But of course Mr Collins, this way please!"

(The bill was settled, and Eddy was very pleased with the costs, and to end the evening they went for a walk and perhaps a last short visit to their favourite coffee bar.)

(The breakfast was served a bit earlier than usual and soon after they were ready to depart. After saying goodbye to Giovanni and family, they thought to pop in at the hotel Riviera for a quick goodbye to John)

"Ready to leave then? Well I expect to see you all in a couple of months, if not before!"

"Thank you uncle for everything John, you have been most kind to let stay here at the hotel pool." **(and so she embraces him with a few tears)**

"Come on, come on... you soapy so and so.. it won't be long before I see you..you are simply a darling, and don't forget do not lose that kind of agreement with Gloria, it's very important that you keep it safe, that it's a very good opportunity for you, you think you are going to have a business by not forking out a single penny, your goodwill is quite enough!"

"Thank you uncle, I will indeed, and thank you for caring about that agreement, I won't lose it I promise, you have a copy anyway, and thank you for giving me a lot of pleasure!"

(Suzanne's father was a bit perplex by the ongoing discussion...God knows what he thought)

"Come here darling Claire, you just look after those two, as I know you are in charge!"

"Not always John, those two they tell me off now and then..ah, ah, ah!"

"Have a safe journey the lot of you....bye..."

(And so that was the end of a beautiful Italian holiday, but for John was the beginning of some more problems)

Chapter 21

(Although not very happy and unwillingly, John went downtown to the police station to donate his finger prints, it didn't take long, and luckily Ispettore Lancini was there too to assist him)

"Thank you for coming, that was quite speedy Mr. Collins, don't worry everything will be alright!"
"Yes it didn't take that long.....I suppose all I have to wait now for the results!"
"That's alright, I shall give you a ring or I shall come to see you personally!"
"Anyway..thank you very Ispettore.. Goodbye…"
"Bye, bye…Mr. Collins!"

(Two days later Suzanne and family arrived safely home, happy to see grandparents Tom and Anne and happy to see the house in good order. They unpack their suitcases and they thought to treat the grandparents to a bite to eat that evening, the five of them went out to the local pub)

"I really craved for this fish and chips Claire, and I see my parents they are loving it too, how about you Suzanne?

"It's alright dad, I suppose I'll get used to it!"
"Here we go, you know something Anne? You give a little taste of good life, and they expect that all the time!"
"Don't worry darling, I know exactly how you feel, these new generation are never happy!"
"But Nan...I am very happy, and more happier now that I've seen you in good form, and you granddad too!"
"there she goes our darling, always full of compliments!"
"We are so glad that you had a wonderful time, sadly our holidays abroad are gone forever...."
"Don't be like that Nan, you still young as ever!"
"Thank you for your compliment too sweetheart...This probably will cost me a new dress when we go shopping!"
"Thank you Nan, I shall remind you that."

(Before going to bed Suzanne thought to make a phone call to Barry, and put his mind at rest)
"Hello....hello...
"Hello..who's that?"
"It's me Suzanne..couldn't you hear my voice?"
"Oh..hello Suzanne...No I didn't recognize your voice, it sounded miles away...like your heart when we were in Italy...Still I never complained ...Did I?""
"NO you never..... you poetic silly sod..I'm back now and look forward to see you, next Monday I shall start to work, can we see each other before then?"
"Of course darling, you know dam well I want to see you!"
"Right then tomorrow afternoon I'm free, I think it would be a good idea to go for a coffee."
"Why not darling, I want to see you so much, actually this distance made me realize that I really love you."
"Well. I don't know so much Barry, but I feel I've been missing you, do you think that I love you too?"

"Well you should know that, you never said such a thing during our two weeks in Italy, I am quite surprise hearing you saying that now."

"Don't be silly Barry, I might not expressed myself as you think I would be, but I feelt for you, in fact I must say that you never tried to express yourself as I would have like you to do!"

"Yes you are right, probably because I was afraid to be rejected, you are so powerful when you speak, that you can crash even my thoughts!"

"I think you are exaggerating a bit Barry, I'm not that powerful as you might think, the fact is that I probably spoke more than you did!"

"That's true Suzanne...Oh.... I look so forward to see you tomorrow, seems ages since we saw each other."

"Look there is a coffer bar in Greatstone high street, it's called "The Expresso" can you meet me at three o/clock in the afternoon?"

"Of course darling, I'll be there...I think my mum is calling me...I'll meet you there then bye, bye darling bye!"

"Bye, ..Barry...bye..."

(Suzanne and Barry they met the next day with a lot of enthusiasm)

"Hi darling how was your journey then?"

"Really, really nice, we stopped at this beautiful small hotel in the middle of France, and don't laugh, there out of the blue we met a couple living in Greatstone."

"Did you know them?"

"Of course we did, the lady is one of my costumer, and my parents knew them as well."

"Were they on holiday in Italy too?"

"No, they have been on holiday in Switzerland, we just couldn't believe it! Anyway we have a drink and a good laugh, yes it was nice to meet someone from our town! how about you Barry, did you have a nice journey back?"
Nothing really fantastic, you know what is like flying, you don't see a sodden thing."
"I see what you mean Barry, have you started to work yet?"
"Not really, next Monday we are erecting a new tower, there's not much brick work involved, but I think I shall have to do my bit."
"I'm so glad that you are helping out you father, and I'm sure he'll appreciate that!"
"He certainly does, but he says if I want to pay for my new car, I've got to work for it like he did when he was my age!"
"And I think he's right, money does not grow on trees.. you know?"
(Barry touching her hand and whisper...."It's so nice to see you again Suzanne, can we meet again? Perhaps next week I'll pick you with my new car and go for a nice meal somewhere."
"That'll be nice Barry.. just give me a call, and we can fix a date, I am off Saturday and Sundays or maybe we can go during the week…what the hell!"
"Yes, I leave it up to you darling… it's okay with me!"
"Alright sweetheart…see you next week then**…(and so they both gently kissed each other…On his way out Barry turned around and waved, and so did Suzanne)**

(Two old ladies were sitting next to them, they remarked; "What a lovely couple! **Suzanne happened to hear them and said…**"Thank you!!"

(Eddy due to start to work the coming Monday, just in case he thought to pay a visit to Jack, to make sure he was back from his holiday, in actual fact he was as he saw the lights shining through his windows)

"Hello Jack, I see you are back too, we arrived yesterday, and I thought to pay you a visit!"

"Please coming Eddy, we are just having a coffee, would you like one?"

"Thank you, I hope I'm not disturbing you at this time, but I thought to make sure that we are starting this Monday coming."

"Of course Eddy, we have quite a few cars to service, they have been awaiting for us to open!"

"That's wonderful news then, better be busy than doing nothing!"

"Yes it's true Eddy! Anyway...during the past three weeks I have been doing some thinking about me stopping to slave myself, and to be honest with you, I have been to the doctor, for some little problems and he told that I have to slow down, I thought sooner or later, this had to happen!"

"I'm so sorry to hear that Jack, so what are you going to do?"

"Well..the first option is probably to sell out, which really I don't want to, as I would have to find another house, and the moving would be too much for me, the second option is that I could hand over the business to you and you could give me a percentage of your takings, now I haven't worked out this at all, but I'm sure it could arranged, what do you think?"

"That isn't a bad idea, but If I would take over I would have to employ another mechanic as on my own I wouldn't be able to cope…"

"True Eddy.. I think this garage needs three workers, not two, at the moment there's only you and I, because you work for two people sometime, I must admit that, you are a dam good worker Eddy!"

"Thank you Jack, I really do appreciate your good words, anyway, you think carefully what you want to do, then me and Mrs. will discuss the situation, and see what happen!"

"I will sit down this weekend and workout what to do, and please don't you worry about your job, for the moment it's quite safe… apart from that; Have you enjoyed your holiday? Is your brother alright? I know he had some problem with his marriage, but I expect that is over now."

"He is okay, he's got a good job, he might come over next month to visit us and probably he will see his ex wife, I think they still cuddle each other now and then….ah, ah, ah, ah! "

"That' s the way to do it…life is too short to bear grudges!"

"Thanks for the coffee Jack and I'll see you on Monday!"

"Thanks for popping around Eddy..I'll see you on Monday! Perhaps I will sort out something by then."

"Thank you again Jack…. ever so much…."

Chapter 22

(Monday morning, a new day, for Eddy's family, as everyone was leaving for work, Suzanne was asked a million questions by her colleagues' at work, as she was the only one amongst them who visited Italy, not only that but the Italian Riviera, most celebrated place to spend your holiday, and the solicitor's people were more than pleased to see Claire back with a beautiful suntan)

"Yes, my uncle is the general manager of a five stars Hotel on the Riviera, don't laugh it's called; the Hotel Riviera, it has three swimming pools, and there we met a family from Littlewood, lovely people with one son called Barry."
"You lucky girl, I bet you spend a few days with this Barry, is he good looking?"
"Yes, he's got quite a macho look, but sometimes he's a bit shy, few days? I'd say we spent every day swimming in the main pool, we met on Saturday at the Expresso coffee bar, and we had a long chat.. we are going out this weekend again, for a bite to eat!"
"Are you going out together then?"
"Well…I think we will, he already told me that he loves me, whether he's serious or not , I don't really know!"

"Did you and him… you know?"

"Helen….? No really, I think the time we spent together, it was purely kind of friendship, although as I said he told me that he likes me very much."

"Gosh, you really got him then, is he from a rich family?"

"I think so, his father has a building company, they build houses , and Barry is a champion brick layer!"

"I wouldn't let him go if I were you, sounds like you got him under your skin."

"Perhaps…..And my uncle was ever so gentle, and you know? He's quite good looking, it reminds me of that first James bond, he's got that savoir fair especially with the ladies!"

"Is he married this uncle of yours…and what's his name?"

"He's divorced, actually his ex wife came here a couple of times, to get a perm done….very good looking lady, and sophisticated, his name is John, and don't laugh.. she was staying in his hotel too for a week… Gloria, yes she's a nice woman, you know something Helen? They are divorced and yet, they are still good friends, I personally think they still love each other….Shsh… I know she spent a few nights in his personal chalet…"

"He's really a James Bond type then Suzanne, I wouldn't mind to meet him."

"I think he's coming to visit us in a couple of months, I might even introduce him to you!"

"Well… I need someone to cheer me up, since that stupid David left me, I haven't had a chance to meet anyone, sometime I feel so miserable, I still cannot believe why David left me, we had such a wonderful life together, and of course I never refused any of his sexual demands, I really thought we were made for each other!"

"Maybe that was the problem… for letting yourself go freely towards him, but of course if you loved him so much, I can understand your kindness!"

"Yes…I did love him very much, and as we made some plans to get married, I didn't think it matter too much, giving what he wanted!"

"I see what you mean Helen, I really feel sorry for you, I think I'm learning something from your past!"

"Yes… be very careful girl, and make sure, you take that little pill, you can avoid a lot of problems with that!"

"Thanks Helen, I'll bear that in mind… I think I better see to that lady, her hair are almost dry…"

"Yes you do that, anyway it's nice to see you back, I say Suzanne, when you see Barry again, ask him if he has a friend, we might make a foursome and go to a disco or maybe to a restaurant, I really need someone to cheer me up…I wonder when….that will happen…."

"Be patient Helen, Rome wasn't built in a day!"

(Meanwhile Eddy was working on a car, at Jack's garage)

"This car is in poor conditions Jack, you'll have to tell its owner that he need to rep[lace its discs breaks, they are quite rusty, and I don't think they would last long, so before I complete the service you better give him a ring!"

"Thank you Eddy, I really don't know what I would do if you weren't here, yes I will ring him…is the chap who owns the grocery shop!"

"Oh…I know him, between you and I Jack, I think he can afford a new car, instead going around with this banger."

"You're so right Eddy, he's been running that shop for years, and he's always moaning about money, I think he's loaded, what a wife and no kids? He certainly is…"

"that's true Jack.. have thought anymore about the future of your garage?"

"Yes Eddy, at the end of the day, I would like to sit down with you and have a proper chat!"

"I hope it's good news Jack…"

"All I can tell you is you won't be disappointed."

"I'm so glad to hear that Jack, my Claire was a bit worried this morning about the outcome, she pointed out that there are not many garages here in Greatstone to look for another job."

"True Eddy, and as long we are one the very few, we will always have enough customers to keep us going."

(Claire is already at home and getting the dinner ready and Suzanne is just about to come through the door)

"Hello darling is that you?"

"Yes mum.. it's me…Oh… what a day I had today, we have been so busy, for sure we could have done with a couple more girls!"

"It mean that hairdresser is getting more busier than ever, perhaps this town could do with another one!"

"Bytheway, we haven't heard from Gloria yet, do you think she changed her mind?"

"Can't tell you darling, I suppose you'll have to give some more time!"

(In that moment the phone rings)

"That must be dad, he's a bit late…maybe he stopped to have a chat with Jack and he wants us to know it!"

"Hello….Oh hello Gloria… how are you? Yes we came back Friday and yes we a lovely and quiet journey back!"

"Oh..I'm so glad to talk to you Suzanne…The reason I'm calling, it's about that new venture of mine, perhaps this weekend you and your parents could come over and have a. chat!"
"But of course Gloria, with pleasure."
"At the same time you can see the premises of the new salon, my dad has done already some drawings where we can put the sinks and the reception desk, and also a little waiting room with a couple of settees, then of course I have my old school friend Gordon, who is qualified as an interior designer, he's been designing shops in London...You know?"
"That's wonderful Gloria, I can see that you got quite busy and you are very determine to accomplish your dream!"
"And another thing Suzanne, come around eleven in the morning, then after our chat we can have a little snack!"
"Yes of course, too kind of you to do that, but we are delighted to accept!"
"So we'll see you Saturday morning then Bye, bye Suzanne…regards to your parents."
"See you then Gloria.. thank you very much!"
(Suzanne tells her mum about Gloria's chat, and they both seem to be very happy indeed)
"Just wait until we'll tell dad, I'm sure he'll be happy to hear the good news…..I think I heard the door opening, oh yes, hello dad….(**And so Suzanne tells her dad the good news from Gloria)**
"That is fantastic Suzanne, perhaps I think I better tell you both the second good news from Jack!"
"Come on dad, don't keep us in suspense…"

"Well…he told me that from the beginning of next month, I can take over his business, all he wants is twenty five per cent of the takings including the rent, he showed me his books, and I think even if I employed two people I still will double my wages, of course the good advantage is that I won't pay any rent, but I shall have to pay the electricity."

"So.. will you have to employ two people?"

"Not really, if I find the right one who knows his job properly, it'll be enough!"

"That is fantastic Eddy..Are you happy about it?"

"Of course I am Claire, Jack let me have that, because he doesn't want to move somewhere else, he's happy in his house, although they have no kids, but he told me that he enjoys a bit of good life, and his garden!"

"Good old Jack, he has been good to you over the years, and now although he's packing up work, he wants you to be happy….bless him..I think we must invite him and his wife for dinner again, we haven't had them for a long time, for that we can show them our appreciation!"

"That's a good idea Claire, you choose the date and tomorrow I'll tell him, and please Suzanne don't make any arrangements, I would like you to be here too!"

"Come on then you too, I made a nice shepherd's pie for dinner and it is ready, we can discuss other things during dinner, and this is for you Eddy to thank you for your careful holiday driving."

"Oh.. a nice bottle of Beaujolais I haven't had that for years, thank you darling, will you have a glass with me?"

"Just half glass, you know I am not a wine drinker, especially when is red and dry!"

"But this one I can assure you that is not very dry, it has a a very gentle bouquet!"

"Listen to him mum..the wine connoisseur!"

"My dear Suzanne I know what I'm talking about!"

(The next day Eddy was in work five minutes earlier)

"Jack… Claire and I have been having a chat about your offer, and we decided, to accept it, with all our thanks and appreciation for your kindness, and of course, we would like you and your dear wife to join us for next Sunday's lunch, please don't say no!"
"I'm sure Doreen will be glad to accept your invitation and so will I, thank you so much Eddy!"
"That's it then, I think I'd better get on with that car Jack!"

(Another day went by and for Suzanne was again another long day, as she was leaving her hairdresser, she noticed Barry was waiting outside)

"Hello darling! What a surprise, have you been waiting long?"
"Not really I knew the time you finished, actually I came to town to do something and I thought to look you up, before going home."
"Thank you… That was a nice thought, anyway, are you working, or are still lazing about.. no offence."
"Of course… I know you don't mean that, but I was thinking Suzanne, are doing anything special this Saturday?"
"Not really, I am free in the evening not at lunch time!"
"Well… how about going out Saturday evening then, tell you what.. I know a nice little restaurant in Littlewood, how about that then?"
"Why not…Yes I would love to, are you going to pick me up from my house or shall I meet you somewhere else?"

"No…You stay put where you are, I shall come and pick you up where you live, in fact you'll have a chance to see my new car, my parents bought it for me on my twenty two birthday."

"When was your birthday then?"

"Actually it was the next day we came home!"

"And you never said anything to me or to anyone else!"

"Well.. you know what I'm like Suzanne, I simply didn't think it was that important!"

"Of course it important, my parents and I could have bought a cake from somewhere, and perhaps have it in that coffee bar we used to meet, after all your parents bought me a cake for my birthday and a bottle of Prosecco!"

"And they were delighted to do it, they like you and your parents a lot."

"Oh…It's nice to hear that, at least when I'll see them again I know they'll be pleased to see me!"

"In fact I was thinking, when we come back to that restaurant, you could just pop in and say hello to my parents…How's that then?"

"Perfect Barry, so it's a date, what time will you pick me up?"

"Say at six thirty, I shall book a table for seven o/clock!"

"That wonderful Barry see you then…bye darling (**giving a peck on his cheek, and him likewise**)

"See you Saturday darling!"

Chapter 23

(That long waited Saturday arrived and of course at eleven am Suzanne and parents arrived at Gloria's house, Eddy and Claire were happy to meet Gloria's parents Amy and Tony again, but Suzanne didn't remember them, nevertheless she was pleased to meet them too. While Amy prepare something to eat, Gloria and her dad took Suzanne and her parents to see the new hairdresser salon)

"This is impressive Gloria, what a lovely room, and the entrance is really beautiful!"
"Just wait until it's finished Suzanne, it will be more than impressive, and also we thought to put a coffee machine in the waiting room so they'll have a free coffee too while they wait!"
"Really, really nice Gloria, what do you think mum? What else is there to say? You said everything, the place is absolutely first class, then of course it very well decorated."
"I couldn't agree more with you all, yes it's beautiful!"
"So...Suzanne do you still accept what's written on that paper?"

"Absolutely Gloria, all we have to now is to set a date for the opening as I shall have to give my notice in."

"But first there's one more important thing to do, is to make an application to our local council for the permission to use those to rooms as business!"

"I hope they won't refuse, you know what they are like them people."

"Suzanne there is not another hairdresser for miles, so we are not breaking anybody else's business, just leave that to my father he knows what to do!"

"I hope everything goes as planned!"

"Don't worry Suzanne, and now let's have a glass of wine to celebrate the new venture, and while we do that we better dream up a name, which personally I thought to call it "Suzanne Salon hair beauty" how's that, appealing?"

"Why not.... Gloria Salon…?"

"No I don't think Gloria would appeal, after all Gloria doesn't know much about hairdressing!"

"Thank you Gloria, I feel somehow to be dreaming!"

"And for the moment Suzanne, don't say a word to anybody, especially your boss, if she knew that, she would certainly do her nut, and perhaps throw you out."

"Only Barry knows it, as he was at the swimming pool when uncle John mentioned it to me, but I am seeing Barry this evening and I will tell him not to mention it to anyone fort the moment!"

"Good, that settle then…..Cheers everyone…cheers!"

(They had something to eat and a couple of glasses of wine, and before they left Suzanne and Gloria signed their kind of agreement in good faith)

"I will ring John this evening and tell him the good news!"
"Give him our kind regards Gloria, and tell him not to work too hard…Bye, bye Gloria see you soon."
"Bye, bye to all of you…"

(Barry arrived punctual in his flashy new car, a silver sporty kind of Japanese make with a sun roof open, Suzanne was ready and saw from her window as he got out of the car…she waved at him and soon after there they were driving to the restaurant in Littlewood)

"I was this morning in Littlewood to visit Gloria, as she show us her new future hairdressing salon!"
"How was it Suzanne…Did you like it?"
"It was really first class, you'll see… Bytheway Barry, can I ask you a favour?"
"Please do darling…."
"Would you be so kind not t say anything about this new venture, because there are a few matter to get strait, before we are certain, furthermore, if my boss will find out I might get the sack."
"Darling, don't worry about that, my lips are completely sealed, unless of course if you allow me to kiss you!"
"I like that Barry, I must say all of a sudden you are opening up, I thought at first you were shy, perhaps I was wrong…."
"Yes I was a bit shy when first I met you, for the simple reason that I thought I could never cope with your beauty and your personality."
"Thank you Barry, you are too kind, I'm just a simple girl from a working family, and that's how I was brought up, some kind of luxuries never existed for me!"

"Neither do I... nor my dad or mum, what they have they had to work hard to get it, that is why my dad showed me how to lay brick, and just looking at them....Here we are Suzanne..."

"What a beautiful place and very rustic."

"Shall we have a table outside on the veranda?"

"Why not darling... we can watch them pigeons kissing each other.."

(They ordered their meal, and they seemed to enjoy every bite of it, but all of sudden Suzanne noticed Gloria with a gentleman, of course Gloria saw them too, and couldn't wait to walk towards Suzanne and Barry's table)

"Hello you two lovers, I seemed to know this good looking chap...am I right?"

"Yes you are right Gloria, and nice to see you too, I've never seen your friend over there!"

"Neither did I Gloria...is he ......"

"Nothing like that Suzanne, actually come to think of it John would be very jealous if he knew he was here with me...Yes Suzanne he is Gordon my interior designer, the one I already mentioned to you...who will decorate our new business, he knows his job alright, and that's what we are discussing between some food and wine, I see you are both drinking coke, would like a glass?"

"No thank you Gloria, I drive and Suzanne doesn't drink wine, although I did offer Suzanne...I say the food here is superb, do you come here often?"

"Oh, yes, this is almost our local... well, I think I better go back to my charming man...don't forget not to tell Barry about him, **(Zipping her lips)**"

"Don't worry Gloria, I've already done that....."
"Good....See you later young lovers...."
"Enjoy your meal Gloria...."
"Thank you...and yours too."

"What a girl that Gloria....eh?
"Yes, she really has her head on her shoulder!"
"I can't understand your uncle....Is he sorry to have divorced her?"
"I think he is Barry, the trouble with my uncle, although is only thirty, he thinks that he still twenty, maybe he hates to take family responsibility, this is probably why they never had any kids during their five years of matrimony, and I think the world of him, he's a very clever man!"
"Not that much if he made a silly mistake going with atoner woman!"
"It's not like that, it was the other woman that pestered him so much that she managed to let Gloria to find out his infidelity, probably he didn't do much, knowing him sometime he's all talk and no do!"
"Gosh... you seem to know a lot about him."
"Yes you probably right, and don't forget that he's part of our family, when he split up with Gloria, he went back to live with his parents, then of course he used to visit us quite a bit, and also he used to help out my father at the garage, he's done many jobs, tell you something he can put his hands on anything!"
Cor... what a man, sounds like a James Bond..."

(Barry asked for the bill, Suzanne offer to go half but he refused)

"I invited you out and it's my duty to pay, just be quite Suzanne..."

"Thank you Barry, you are ever so kind, that was a lovely meal I really did enjoy it, I noticed that Gloria is gone already, pity I would have liked to say bye, bye!"

"Never mind darling, you'll see her again soon!"

"yes, no doubt I will, in fact she told me that next week she would like to see all the prices we charge where I work now!"

"She's right about that, she doesn't want to charge more than any other hairdresser,. just because her premises' looking better and new!"

(After saying hello to Barry's parents, who they were over the moon to see Suzanne again...They arrived back at Suzanne's house and she asked him if he wanted to say hello to her parents, he declined as didn't want to disturbed them.)

"Thank you Suzanne for the lovely evening, can I see you again next week?

"Of course darling, you just named the day...perhaps one evening you can come to see me here at home and you can have a chat with my parents, and maybe we can watch a bit of telly!"

"That's not a bad idea Suzanne and you know something?"

"Not really...what?"

"I love you Suzanne..Yes I love you Suzanne, maybe I say it the wrong way.....**(and so they kissed each other very fondly as if they never kissed before)** Yes I do love you Suzanne....I'll ring tomorrow evening.... Bye darling!"

"Please do darling...I love you too, don't forget! Thank you Barry for the lovely evening, bye."

(Suzanne parents were still up watching the telly)

"Hello mum, hello dad…watching a good film?"

"Yes darling… did you have a nice evening with Barry?"

"Really, really nice mum, we went to this restaurant in Littlewood and guess who was there?"

(And so she tells them about Gloria)

"Maybe it's true that she was with her Interior designer, as she has to make that place really first class."

"I wonder whether she needs that, it must cost her a fortune!"

"If that is what she wants, why not, her father can afford it! Just look at the house they live in!"

"Yes it is nice, it's big enough for three families, I wonder why uncle John left her…"

"Let me get this straight Suzanne, he did not leave her, he just got thrown out, just because….just because…..of his idiot fancy women!"

"Alright Claire…alright…That is my brother you are talking about!"

"So what Eddy? are you telling me that he's not an idiot?"

"Well…Claire, I'm not saying that, is that in life we all make mistakes…"

"While you are arguing I'm going upstairs in my bedroom to watch a bit of telly…."

"Yes you do that Suzanne, and I'm going upstairs to read my book and have an early night..Goodnight all!"

"Goodnight dad, hope you enjoy the end of the film!"

"Goodnight the both of you too…love you both"

Chapter 24

(Sunday was a quiet day, Claire was cooking the lunch, Eddy was cutting the grass in their big garden and Suzanne was just about to get up and have a shower)

"What's wrong with your mower Eddy?"

"I don't know, it won't start the dam thing…"

"I think you ought to buy a new one, you had that for donkeys years.!

"I suppose you are right Claire, I keep repairing it, one of these days, won't even be good for the scrap iron man!"

"Lunch will be ready in half an hour, you better give Suzanne a shout, I hope she's not still in bed."

"Just had a shower mum, I'll be down in a minute…"

(They enjoyed their lunch enormously, and then they all relaxed in the garden with a nice coffee)

"This is good life Claire, not too many problems, and a good job to go back tomorrow, which I love doing, what else a man of my age would want to have then?"

"A few more pounds they won't hurt anybody Eddy!"

"Darling, money is not everything, be happy and keep smiling…"

"Yes darling, I can see you enjoy your Sunday lunch and you few glasses of wine…"

(Sunday was certainly a nice sunny day and a very quiet day in England, but down in Italy at the Hotel Riviera, things were quite different, in fact John had another visit from Ispettore Lancini)

"Good morning Ispettore Lancini, I certainly didn't know that you work on Sunday too.... what can I do for you?"
"Good morning Mr. Collins, yes, Unfortunately I do work on Sunday, sometimes I work seven days a week, when we have something important to solve....Anyway... do you think we could have a chat in private?"
"Of course Ispettore…this way please, let's go in my office!"
"Many thanks Mr. Collins, well I'm afraid but I've got some bad news for you, in fact it happens that they found your finger prints on the little plastic bag that contained the drugs which they found in Luca Vanni's car, as he wasn't a drug addict or else he never took any of the stuff, it mean that little bag was planted in his car, of course as I said, they found your finger prints on it, you probably planted it. Did you really?"
"Well Ispettore, I must admit, yes it was me, the truth is that he treat me so badly, yes, I would say sometimes like a piece of shit, excuse my language but it's true."
"Alright we got that story now, and would you mind to tell me who supplied you the drugs?"
"Well…yes, at the time when I was assistant to Mr Vanni, I was also in charge to employ staff at my discretion, as you know summer is quite difficult to get staff.

"Yes I do understand that Mr. Collins...and then?"

"In that period I needed a chap around the pool to do various jobs and luckily this small chap appeared, Of course, I offered him that job, the same day he asked me for an advance in money, as he said he had to find a bed for the night, I told him I couldn't give him any money, but I offered him for one night only to sleep in one of our small changing rooms by the pool."

"Did you have a bed in that changing room?"

"Yes, it had some beach beds in it, and told him he could use one, so he worked all day...and..."

"And then what happened Mr. Collins?"

"Yes... then he slept in that room and in the morning he was nowhere to be found, I search is room and under his bed I found that plastic containing the drug....Obviously he must dropped it and kicked it under the bed."

"And you then thought to use it to incriminate Mr. Vanni.!"

"Well to be honest with you I did not think that such move on mine would cause terrible situation as it turned out to be, believe me!"

"But he did, not only with the authorities, but also with the hotel management, whom dismissed him from his job, and that caused him a lot of pain and depression!"

"Well...I'm so sorry about that, I wish I could turn the time back, and stand up to his nastiness, he was quite brute most of the times to me and some of the staff. He was like a tyrant.. what a nasty fellow, why Oh why some people must behave like that, I just don't kno!"

"That is something you ought to say in front of the magistrate, then you might get a lenient sentence!"

"Of course I will Ispettore, people like that should not be allowed to run businesses, My boss never knew that!"

"Pity...I think if your boss knew that things would have been differently conducted

"Yes Ispettore you are so right....Don't really look forward to go to prison, that would mean losing my job, as I could be classed as a criminal, and you know very well that I am not...mind you this farce makes feel like that!"

"The other choice would that you could make an offer for a settlement out of court, if you do this, your case would still come out in the open, in this case, what would be your boss reaction then?"

"I don't think he would like it very much, I might lose my job, but that would be better than prison."

"Just wait until the case comes up, then you can talk to Mr. Vanni's solicitor!"

"Why can't I talk to him before, if is not pressing charges we don't have to go to court?"

"Maybe, but his solicitor has to inform the magistrate, who will put you on his register, without appearing."

"Does it mean that I will be in the local press?"

"Maybe…Most likely I should think!"

"But if I'll go in the news, I will lose my job, is there anything you can do about it?"

"I'm afraid Mr. Collins, it's not in my power to stop that, the newspapers have the right to report any wrong doing!"

"So what happens now?"

"I shall have to report your admission to Mr. Vanni's solicitor, perhaps I shall ask him to contact you, as I might say that you thought to play a joke on Mr. Vanni, but you were to scare to admit that, and I shall say that you are very sorry, to be quite honest, now that I know the truth, I want this to comes to an end, perhaps you might offer a compensation, I guess the judge will probably order to pay him like that... anyway."

"Anyway, thank you Ispettore, I'm glad you are not arresting me."

"Don't worry we have worst people than you to arrest...if there are changes I will let you know Mr. Collins. Bye.."

"Goodbye Ispettore...and thank you very much!"

(John became really worried, in fact even his staff realized that, as he wasn't himself at all....Then few days later Mr. Vanni's solicitor rung him)

"Hello..My name is Mr. Fiori Mr. Vanni's solicitor.. Am I speaking to Mr. Collins?"

"Yes... hello Mr. Fiori, can I help you?"

"Yes, Ispettore Lancini was telling me that you would like to make some kind of compensation to Mr. Vanni!"

"Yes of course, that would avoid time and bitterness on both sides!"

"Of course, after all no one has been murdered..So what have you got in mind Mr. Collins!"

"Well I was thinking to give him five thousand euro and a very sincere apology!"

"I will pass this on to Mr. Vanni, and see what he says, if he accept, you know, I will have to tell the Magistrate too."

"Okay then Mr. Fiori, I shall wait for you to call me!"

"I will probably call you tomorrow Mr. Collins, bye for now."

"Goodbye Mr. Fiori and thank you!"

(That made John a little happier, after all five grand was almost the amount he got from Roberto's death, plus two grand from Gloria and another ten grand from his wages, which he saved over the past six months as a general manager. That wasn't bad.......

.... and of course, all that didn't put him out of pocket, but he was worried about his job, if his boss found out) (The next day Mr. Fiori rung him)

"Hello .....Good morning Mr. Collins..Mr.Fiori here!"
"Oh... Hello Mr. Fiori... what's the verdict then?
"Mr. Vanni said that he was off work for two months and he reckon he lost six thousand euro during that time, if you accept that, I will come and collect the money!"
"That's okay by me, but I would rather give him the cash myself and ask him to sign such compensation, so I would be able to shake his hand too and apologize!"
"That is nice of you Mr. Collins, so I will arrange a meeting for the three of us!"
"That's very kind of you, please do that, and let me know when and where!"
"Okay the I'll speak to you soon...Bye..."
"Thank you Mr. Fiori...Bye...."

(Really and truly John did not trust anyone when dealing with money, that's the reason he wanted to hand over the money to Vanni, of course he knew that he was not an honest man himself, but he thought to be better and honest than anybody else. In saying that, the next day his solicitor rung up, to try and fix a meeting for the three)

"I don't think the hotel it's the best place to meet Mr. Fiori, there too many people looking and listening!"
"What do you suggest then?"
"I think we should meet in the Blue Seas coffee bar opposite the harbor, about eleven tomorrow morning!"
"That's fine with me Mr. Collins..see you then.."

"Thank you Mr. Fiori, don't forget the two copies of receiving heading letter, for us to sign!"
"I won't don't worry!"

(John was ten minutes earlier and thought to have a coffee, Vanni and his solicitor arrived, they both signed the papers and shake hands, John handed the envelope to the solicitor, he confirmed that the money was okay, Vanni didn't say a lot, he seemed to be a bit cool, John asked them if they wanted a drink or perhaps a coffee.
but Vanni refused by saying he had to go somewhere else, and so they left, leaving John a little perplexed, but he was happy to have his piece of paper signed by settling his debt. What else could have gone wrong now? So he walked back to the hotel.
John wasn't very happy about Vanni attitude, but there was nothing he could do, he certainly had to pay a high price for what he had done, considering that he liberated the staff from a tyrant. Yes, Luca Vanni was not a nice person he treated everyone like dirt, and of course he treated John like shit sometime, but patiently he put up with him, as he didn't want to lose his job, which he cared about and he cared about the staff, he was working with as they worked hard to earn their leaving. Everyone who knew John, thought he was good but some kind of playboy, not so much, he was good hearted and always appreciated good people)

Chapter 25

(Few days' gone by and back in England the new Hairdresser salon, was taking shape, so Gloria invited Suzanne, to go and see the new premises, hoping to get some good suggestions)

"What do you think Suzanne?"

"Absolutely fabulous.. perhaps I would put a sliding door between the waiting room and the salon, just to shut off the smell of the sprays, sometime they can be quite strong, especially if you are having a coffee!"

"Good thinking Suzanne, so glad you came, that's what I like, working together, two brains are better than one!"

"You are certainly right, but you have done miracles!"

"It wasn't only me darling, I think my interior designer deserve some credits, he's a very clever man, you know that he created some of the most famous salon in London?"

"How interesting, I didn't have a look at him properly when I saw you in the restaurant, as he had his back turned on us!"

"Mind you, I offered him to come and meet you, but he decline, I think he's a bit shy, but very sophisticated."

"He's not the other way Gloria…is he?"

"I don't think so Suzanne, in school we were very close and enjoyed our friendship a lot, many time I thought he fancied me, and now I can only say that we only discussed business, and nothing else!"

"Yes Gloria this is really nice, bytheway, have you heard from the council for the change of use?"

"Yes, all is in order..."

"Any idea of the opening day? You know we'll have to have a little welcoming party with a few drinks and bits and pieces, I know quite a few of my customers that we could invite!"

"Do you think that would be feasible? I don't want to hurt any other business, or I would say stealing their customers."

"Well.. perhaps if you feel that way, I will agree with you, maybe we could pop through house's doors nice leaflets with some photographs, with the date of opening and various prices, so people coming they would know where they stand with their pocket!"

"That is a fantastic idea Suzanne, but we must be slightly cheaper than most!"

"Of course Gloria, but let's not make prices too cheap, and the other thing I shall have to give my boss a couple of weeks notice."

"I expect to start in three or four weeks, so I would think you can give your notice in next week perhaps, we'll probably need a few days practicing, with some of my friends, my mum, your mum, then we'll need another assistant, anyone you know?"

"My neighbor have a daughter who just left school, she'd be just right for the job, as an apprentice!"

"Why don't you offer her to come and join us, it will be a good opportunity for her, as she just left school, and I'm sure her parents will be glad to know she's leaning a profession!"

"Perfect I will, and next time I come to see you, I'll bring her with me, at the same time I will find out how much my boss pays the apprentices, further more I think he get a government allowance on those!"

"That's fantastic..I'm so glad that you are joining me, I'm sure we can do great things!"

"I'm sure we will Gloria, we can only try, bytheway, have you heard from my uncle."

"Yes,... only once, and not for long as he was very busy, you know him, always running about!"

"Yes I do Gloria...So that's it then, I'll give you a ring next week, and let you know about my notice, and see if that girl wants the job, in the meant bye, bye!"

"That's perfect darling, and thanks for coming, you have been absolutely great with full of brilliant ideas, bye, bye.

(Suzanne was very excited about the new venture and very happy about the look of the new salon, and so, she was telling her mum)

"I'm so pleased for you Suzanne, I think a new environment will do you good, and if that doesn't work, you don't have to worry about it, as you are not losing anything, plus you still have your profession!"

"Thank mum, that's true. Gloria and I we were thinking to employ an apprentice, you know washing hair making coffee, sweeping the floor and so forth, what do you think if I would ask Tracy next door? She just left school and I heard she was looking for a job!"

"I'm sure she would love that, after all they are not a well off family, yes, later on just go over and offer her the job, and see what she says."
"Good, I will do that..she's a lovely girl!"

(Back in Italy at the Hotel Riviera, John had a phone call from his boss Mr. Rocco, saying that he wanted to see him. John started to worry, thinking about Vanni's problem, he thought as far as he knew he saw nothing in the local newspaper, and so he was wondering. The next day John was behind the reception desk dealing with a customer, when all of a sudden he saw Mr. Rocco coming in)

"Good morning Mr. Rocco, I'll be with you in a few minutes, please go into my office, I will send you a coffee."
"No.. John, I don't need a coffee, and don't be long as I must attend a meeting!"
"Just a few minutes Mr. Rocco!"
"Just hurry up, I've got time to waist, for goodness sake…"
(The customer who John was dealing with was rather annoyed and embarrassed, looked at Rocco and shake his head, then he looked ad John and said…)
"Excuse me John, I've been here twice in the past few months, and never met a chap behaving like that, without even say; sorry to interrupt or even please...Who is he anyway that bloody cheeky and unspoilt chap?"
"Well...Signor Comini he's Mr. Rocco the big Boss...of this hotel"
"What?? And he's behaving like that??
"Well...Yes Mr. Comini, he was well out of order...!

"Yes he was indeed John.....You tell him from me that he shouldn't behave like a small boss in front of a paying customer, you do that John, go on, go and see him, I'll be waiting here just outside that door, you can finish with me later!"

(John did exactly what Mr. Comini suggested)

"Yes Mr. Rocco, what can I do for you…."

"Just look here, I received this letter from Luca Vanni, and he tells me what you have done to him."

"Yes, that was done as a joke, in a manner of speaking, as Luca has been a terrible manager for this hotel, he treated the staff like dirt and he treated me like shit, I paid him a high price for that…. did he tell you how much?"

"No he didn't…What price?

"Six thousand euro….. and you come in here upsetting my customers and me in a very abrupt manner and without hesitation, what sort of a boss are you?"

(Mr. Comini was just outside the door listening, and all of a sudden he opened the door and…..)

"Yes what kind of a boss are you rudely interrupting your manager and a good paying customer…John get my bill ready, I will not stay one minute later in this joint, not with some spoiled brat like him!"

"Sorry Mr. Comini, I'll be with you in a minute…."

"Oh no… you come and do my bill first, and leave that charlatan waiting, he doesn't know how to behave in life, and may I remind you small boss that he's been making his money with people like me and tell him to shut up"

"How do you dare to talk about me like that?"

"YES….You shut up Rocco, now I am busy doing his bill, you can talk to me later when I have time, if you don't like it you can stick your job up yours……and run this joint yourslf..."

"But….but….but…."

"But my arsh……."

(John and Mr. Comini went out of the door, leaving Rocco on his own, speechless)

"Good John, that will teach him a lesson he will never forget in his life, and here's my card John, I run quite a few businesses, if you need a job just give me a ring!"

"Thank you Mr. Comini, I think I shall probably need a new job after that excited commotion."

"Don't worry John, I think people like him need to be told how to behave in life!"

"Thank you Mr. Comini, I didn't really want you to drag you into this, I would like to say bye, bye, before you leave!"

"You will John, please send the porter up to get my luggage, in an hour!"

"Yes I will sir…."

(John went back to the office and saw his boss with his head down, looking at a chart laying on his desk)

"Yes that is a chart of new arrivals, we are going to be full up for the four weeks coming, if you like to get a new manager you are welcome, but don't forget that my contract expire in two months, so I'll be grateful if you fulfill your obligation to settle our agreement!"

"John I didn't come here to sack you, I really wanted some answers about this letter!"

"Yes you had them, if Vanni was an honest person he would have say that also a deal was done through his solicitor and me for that payment, after all he deserved for what he's done over this past few years, just look at the chart how many workers have left because of his nastiness, go on... have look at this **(showing the chart)** and hardly any left since I took over….Right?"

"Yes I can see that, so what are we going to do?"

"Well, I finish my contract and then I'll go, or else you pay me in full for the rest two months and you can stand behind that desk yourself Rocco, until you find a decent manager!"

"Well John no need to get so hasty, shall we say that I never received this letter?"

"Oh no… You write back to Vanni and tell him what I say; His agreement with me was legal, and his letter is illegally infamous, and tell him that I will see my solicitor now and demand a compensation exactly like he did, in the meantime don't worry Rocco, I will see that your Hotel is run how it should be…

"Of course, I will see that my reply is sent to him today, and you will get a copy of it!"

"Thank you....And you can have a copy of Vanni and myself agreement signed in front of his solicitor, and please can I have a copy of the one he has sent to you?"

"Of course John …here just make a copy of it…Bloody hell, as you say, he never mentioned anything like that, he can't be a very clever chap..and he was my manager?!"

"Unfortunately Rocco he was, pity you never knew him well, now if you excuse me.... I am very busy. Hope to see you soon..goodbye…!"

"You will John don't worry…Bytheway, will you please convey my apologies to Mr. Comini, tell him I was really out of order…..goodbye!"

"I certainly will..."

"Hi John I put Mr. Comini suitcases in the small room, just give me a shout when he comes down!"

"Okay Luigi, thank you very much, tell me has he been kind to you…? You know what I mean!"

"Yes…. he gave me twenty euro, he's a good customer, but he told me he's not very happy about the big boss!"

"Oh yes Luigi, but now everything seemed to have gone my way, I will control the big boss from now on, I know exactly how to handle him!"

"I like you John and thank you for letting me call you John and not Mr. Collins…."

(Mr. Comini came downstairs soon after, and as he collected his luggage John told him what happened with his boss, Mr. Comini was quite happy to hear about the apologies, John was more grateful for his intervention, which helped him to sort out the problem.)

(Two days later John gets a phone call from Luca Vanni)

"Good morning John, Luca's speaking… Now look I really didn't mean to send a letter to Rocco, I just don't know why I've done it, I do apologize about that, I hope you will understand."

"Now look here Luca, I made a mistake playing that joke to you, but I did put it strait by giving you the money you asked legally, I didn't have to, if we went to court and fight it, you would have lost, as I would have said how bad you treated the staff here at the hotel and myself…You know dam well that is the truth.. and now you had the cheek to send a letter to Rocco, hoping to get me the sack, it didn't work like that, as I explained Rocco the real truth, so now I want my six thousand Euros back or I will take you to court for infringement of our legal agreement.

"But John I did apologized to you, you can't do that!"

"Oh yes I can, you try me, now I'll give you a couple of days, get my money back here or else, if you don't want to bring it yourself , ask your solicitor to bring it, and that it will cost you more money!"

"I think you are very unfair John.!

"I don't think I am, you are the one very nasty and unfair, you made a bigger mistake than me!"

"I must tell you that I lost my last job too, and if I give you back that money, I will be penniless!"

"That's your problem Luca, and let me guess, you lost your job because you are a tyrant with the workers....Yes?"

"So I have been told, but I am changing now!"

"Make sure you change you attitude and bring back my money, by tomorrow, otherwise you'll hear from my solicitor...Thank you for ringing, bye"

"Bye…. John, bye…"

Chapter 26

(Back in England Suzanne was taking young Tracy to meet Gloria and to talk about her new job)

"Hello Gloria..... Please meet Tracy our future new recruit, I hope she will like.... what she sees!"
"Hello Suzanne and hello Tracy, so nice to meet you, please come in...."
"Oh thank you Miss Gloria, and nice to you too."
"Please Tracy...here we are all friends, and there's no need to address me as Miss...Just Gloria please! Now then, as you can see this is where we make all the ladies beautiful, your job to start with is washing their hair, and make some tea or coffee and a few other jobs, don't worry we will not force you to do anything that you are not able to do, you will work five days a week, for the first week you will be on trial, with pay of course, you will get paid eight pound per hour to start and depend how good you are we will increase it accordingly. What do you think Tracy, is the job suitable for you?"
"Many thanks, Yes...I am all excited, I want so much to learn this trade..."

"Right my darling I think we said it all, if you have any questions please don't be afraid, as I said before we are all equals here!"

"I am sure I'll be very happy Gloria, thank you both of you to give me this chance, I really appreciate it!"

"I'm so glad Tracy, Suzanne will let you know when to start…"

"Thank you Gloria I think we better go back home now, see you soon then, bye, bye!"

"Bye, bye Suzanne…Bye Tracy…take care!"

(Few days later back in Italy, John was still waiting for Luca to bring the money back but unfortunately no sign of him, he thought to ring his house as he still had his phone number from the old days)

"Hello Vanni residenza speaking…"

"Oh... hello Signora..could I speak to Luca please?"

"Who is that speaking?"

"This is John Signora from the Hotel Riviera, he was supposed to come and see me, but he didn't turned up!"

"I' very sorry, but Luca is in bed, he's not feeling very well!"

"Maybe you should tell him to ring me back, if I don't hear from him, tomorrow morning I shall go to the police to report him about an infringement of fraud!"

"So sorry Signor John, but he never said anything to me about that!"

"I think you better ask him about that, I'm sure he'll be able to explain... Please signora tell him, I don't want to cause him more bigger troubles than he has..bye, bye...."

"Bye, bye signor John...Please don' t go to the police I must tell you that he's in trouble as it is!"

"Why.... has he done something else I don't know?"

"He was accuse of altering some money from his computer in work, meaning a large sum of it mislaid, he says he hasn't done it, and the police had no choice but to put him under house arrest!"

"Excuse me signora, don't be offended but, your husband is not only a thief, and liar, but he's also a tyrant with people who worked for him, and most of all... he's good for nothing. He stole from me six thousand Euros, and tell him I want my money back by tomorrow or he'll be more in trouble than he is!"

"He never mentioned your problem to me before, and I'm sorry to hear all that. Just leave that to me Signor John, I promise you!"

"Thank you Signora...I'm sorry but I don't know your name!"

"My name is Lucia...Lucia Sarti!"

"I see you are not carrying his surname then?"

"In Italy the wife do not take the husband surname, and thank god for that!"

"I can see you are proud of your surname Signora Sarti!"

"Yes I am, and may I tell you that I don't really know why I'm still married to a bastard like Luca, even his own family don't want to know him!"

"I'm sorry to hear that Signora Sarti, I sincerely hope to meet you one of these days!"

"You will Signor John....You will...bye, bye for now!"

"Goodbye Signora Sarti, and please don't forget to tell him to phone me!"

"Don't worry John..I will... rest assure of that, and please in future address me as Lucia, as I've called you John!"

"Thank you Lucia. it was nice to speak to you!"

(The next day John was down at the pool giving some instructions to a new member of the staff, when is mobile phone rung)

"Mr. Collins there's a nice lady in the reception hall, who would like to talk to you!"
"I'll be up in a minute Jean, ask her to sit in the waiting room!"
"I will Mr. Collins..."

(Five minutes later John appeared in the waiting room, he saw the nice lady who was sitting, looking at a brochure... she looked very smart, very beautiful and elegantly dressed, with long blond hair and blue eyes, in the mid thirties.....John was quite amazed, knowing his good taste in beautiful ladies, actually as he started to talk, he couldn't take his eyes off of her eyes.)
"Good morning.... ehm... what can I do for you?"
"Good morning are you the Signor John I spoke on the phone yesterday?"
"Yes...Let me guess.. you are Signora Sarti..."
"Indeed I am, and nice to meet you, is there a place where we can have a bit more privacy?"
"Of course Signora...Please come to my office.."
"First of all let me tell you that when I told my husband about your phone call, he shrugged his head and said; that he didn't have any money, and he added; let him wait."
"That wasn't very nice Signora Sarti, but I am not surprise knowing what kind of man he is... your husband!"
"Yes you are right Signor John, but he is the kind of man that he couldn't give a toss for anyone, all he thinks is about himself, he's selfish and very hard hearted!"

"Yes indeed Signora Sarti, as far as I know he never had a good word for anyone doing a good job for him."

"It's true Signor John, I think we cannot say more for a brute like him....... Lovely office you have here."

"You mean to tell me that you never been in this office? Surely your husband must have shown you around this place when he was in charge!"

"You must be joking Signor John, he was here for over a year and he never ask me to come here even for a coffee!"

"That's typical Luca...as you said; very selfish indeed!"

"Yes, that's his way of treating people like dirt, but I had enough of him, as soon as I will pay you back your money, I will ask him for a divorce, in the meantime please take this envelope, it contains four thousand Euros, and I hope to get hold of the other two with a bit of luck, as I know that he has quite a few hidden away somewhere in the house, I found these in a sock in the bottom of his desk!"

(As she handed over the envelope John could see that she had tears in her eyes)

"Thank you Signora Sarti, I do appreciate your honesty and please there's no need to get too emotional, (Giving her his top pocket handkerchief to dry her eyes) there are worst things happen at sea!"

"Thank you...silly me.....What do you mean by that Signor John?"

"Just an old English saying...Signora, and please don't call me Signor, just John will do!"

"You too John, I must say you are kind and a very pleasant gentleman, I really mean that!"

"And you are a very pleasant and beautiful lady, what else can a single man like me say?"

"Are you single then?"

"Yes, unfortunately after a turbulent divorce, my ex wife leaves in England, and as you can see, for the moment I live here, in your beautiful country!"

"Yes it is a beautiful country, and I do love it myself....But why Italy? Surely there many better opportunities in England for a young man like you..?"

"Yes there are, but after the earthquake of my marriage, I thought a change of air would do me good...Would like a drink or a coffee Lucia?"

"A coffee will be just fine thank you..."

(John just popped out of the office to order the coffee at the same time he looked in the envelope, yes the money was there.. and back he was in the office)

"That is kind of you John, now I know why Luca never introduced me to you!"

"I don't understand Lucia, I know he was quite unfriendly, as he never mixed with colleague or staff, and I know for a fact he never talk about friends, in fact he never talk that much to me, considering that I was is understudy or assistant, I mean second in command, no one of the workers liked him, they called him; Meinkamp...did he have any friends within his private and sociable life?"

"Not really John, our social life was zero, and he is very jealous, he would do his nut if a man would pay me a compliment, so our sex life became very dull and cold, in fact I'll be honest I can stand to sleep in the same bed as him, and he knows that, and yes he becomes more and more possessive. Yes, Meinkamp, just the name that a nasty fellow deserve!"

"I'm very sorry to hear that Lucia, you life must be hell living with a chap like that!"

"It is indeed John, I'm just waiting to get rid of him for good, sometimes he scares me!"

"Bloody hell...there must be something wrong with his brains, have you told anyone about this?"

"Yes, my family knows everything, in fact some nights I sleep in my parents house, and I have to tell him that my mum or my dad are not well!"

"I suppose that it's a good excuse Lucia...I shouldn't ask you this, but can we meet for coffee somewhere soon? I find it fascinating talking to you.... I do feel somehow a new person, after what I went through with my marriage!"

"Of course John, why not tomorrow...Luca has to go for an interview in Rome, it's so far away that he has to stay for the night in a hotel, I reckon he'll be back the next day, he did asked the police permission for that."

"I suppose because of his job they gave it to him. Well... can we meet at the Cappuccino coffee bar which is situated on the sea front?"

"That's fine by me John...Your coffee is not bad either...tell you what, I enjoyed chatting with you too, I feel more liberated from the nasty thoughts that went through my mind in the past few days... I really hope he gets that job in Rome and good riddance!"

"Lucia, thank you for the money, I do appreciate your concern, which of course it's not your problem, but...!"

"Thank you for your good words John, you might think that it's not my concern, but it's the reputation of my marriage!"

"I understand Lucia...shall we say about four pm tomorrow then?"

"I shall look forward John, thank you for the coffee.. see you tomorrow **(shaking his hand)**

"See you tomorrow Lucia....**(looking in her eyes with an smiling look)**

(Lucia left John with a smile in her eyes, that spoke a thousand words, for certain he knew that a warm attraction was in both hearts)
(John thought to himself) "Bloody hell... just can't believe that.. what a beauty, that Luca must be nuts to neglect a woman like that.... Well...I will see what happens! (In the meantime he was counting the money)** Yes...they are all here...four grand!"

(Next afternoon John was quite early at the Cappuccino coffee bar, as he was reading the newspaper he saw a beautiful hand pulling down the paper from his hidden face. Yes..... it was Lucia)
"Good lord... You made me jump Lucia.. Thank you for coming darling.....Hoops sorry, I didn't mean that....!"
"Don't worry John...I will take that as a compliment, as I didn't get many lately..."
"Thank you...what can I get for you?"
"As I am in a cappuccino bar I shall have a cappuccino!"
"And I will join you with another one...Thank you for coming, is Luca gone to Rome then?"
"Yes, he's gone early this morning, I took him to station with my car, at lunch time he rung me and said that he will have to stay overnight!"
"Did he say why?"
"Yes because the people he's seeing are not back until tomorrow!"
"So you never been at the Hotel Riviera, when he was in charge then?"
"Never, once I asked him if I could use the hotel swimming pool, he told me that only the hotel guests were allowed to use it!"

"That's not true Lucia, my brother and his family were down here a few weeks ago and I allowed them to use it..Why don't you come and use it tomorrow afternoon, I shall give you a pass, actually I've got one here, please take it!"

"I will if you don't mind John."

"Fantastic then, come and relax in the sun for a few hours please, come around eleven then we'll have a little lunch at the pool restaurant!"

(They carried on chatting, and both they seemed to find quite a lot of things to say...to each other"

"I enjoyed chatting to you John, that was wonderful, I will accept yopur invitation..with pleasure... see you tomorrow morning...Bye, bye John."

"Thank you Lucia...see you tomorrow..Bye, bye!"

Chapter 27

(Lucia was at the pool just after eleven, laying on her cosy sun bed, she was reading a book and that didn't last for long as John appeared with a couple long refreshing drinks..)

"Good morning sweet lady, I bet you are thirsty in this hot sun, mind you I am too, as I've been up since six am!"

"Good morning sweet gentleman...if you don't mind I'm paying you the compliment, not only in words, but also in Euros (**Handing over an envelope**) You will find that the rest of your money is there John, and that's my promise is fulfil, you can count them...!"

"No darling I trust you, and what can I say? Thank you very much, you save us both a lot of bother and to make solicitors richer! You don't mind me asking you, was it hidden under the floor?"

"Not really, but I know more or less where he hides it, his problem is that he hides in different places, and sometimes he forgets where he put it."

"Not only you are beautiful Lucia, but also a very clever girl...Really...when I think that us macho men believe we are superior than women...Well it's a joke, is isn't it?"

"Yes it is...And..."

"And what Lucia, please tell me I'm all ears!"

"If you only knew how many times I fooled him, not sexually... but in other ways, you would not believe it, and..He thinks he's the clever one, that's a laugh!"

"I do believe you darling...Cheers to you good health, and naturally, I hope you'll get rid of that scoundrel!"

"Thank you darling...don't worry, it won't be long, while I organize my divorce I'm busy making a list of the nasty things that he did to me and making him pay for it, he just doesn't know what's coming to him."

"Please don't forget to include mine as well!"

"Yours will come at the end, for the final coup!"

"Ah, ah, ah, ah...I like that Lucia...Shall we go and have some lunch, I'm rather peckish!"

"Me too darling...!"

(They had a lovely lobster salad, with a couple of glasses of white wine...)

"Would you like another glass of white wine Lucia?"

"No..Thank you John that was absolutely perfect, in this heat drinking too much alcohol is not good for you, that's why in Italy most of the people mix wine with mineral water I really enjoyed that, and thank you for introducing me to your chef as your sister....Mind you he couldn't take his eyes of me!"

"I don't blame him, he's a single chap too!"

"Lucky fellow....I haven't had a lobster for donkeys years, I think last time it was...let me think , Oh yes... in Marbella with my parents when I was a sweet sixteen virgin."

"Cor.. you must have been some girl even then, I wish I met you then!"

"Pity..But can you do?"

"Nothing much really, I probably was eating fish and chips with my parents... with a cup of tea!"

"Yes I heard that your fish and chips are very well known but I still prefer a glass of wine with fish instead of a cup of tea!"

"Mind you Lucia, the English people are changing style now, almost every family get acquainted with a glass of wine with their meals!"

"I suppose they follow the European style!"

"Very true darling....Anyway, have you got any plans going after your divorce?"

"I might look around for the right man who I would truly love, and be very careful not to get myself a Pratt like my husband, who between you and I... he can hardly climb into bed without falling asleep!"

"Your shoulders are quite red Lucia, I think you should put some sun cream on them, you don't want to be burnt."

"You are right John, but I haven't got any with me, what do you suggest?"

Well I got some in my chalet, which is just around the corner, would you like me to go and get it?"

"Better still I'll come with you, we don't want any nosey parkers seeing the manager putting cream on a guest!"

"I think you are right there Lucia, please come!"

"Christ....you lucky so and so...this is beautiful, what a shame it's got something missing!"

"What is missing then Lucia?"

"Well darling... a girl like me....please John kiss me, I want you so much.."

"But Lucia, what about the cream, put that on too, where ever you like I don't mind... Oh I love you so much John, please, please.....have you locked the door?"

"Of course I did, what do you take me for?"

(Nothing could stop them to get what they really wanted, a passionate love was certainly not a miss)

"Thank you darling that was   wonderful.........No one would believe that a simple phone call from a stranger would have given me such pleasure......This is going to be the best summer day of my life!"

"Mine too darling.....I love you too...God.... where have you been all this time"

"Please don't say another word, just put the cream on!"

(Back in England, Gloria was instructing her Interior designer Gordon, for the final little jobs and of course talking about the days of the   high school days, they were really very much in love then, in fact her parents thought they were going to get married, but that never materialized, instead she married John and Gordon is still single. Of course now she has been using him to do the salon, who he has done a good job so far.)

"Yes, Gloria I think you need more space for your gadgets, I will do exactly as you say."

"Thank you darling, and I think you have done a superb work, which deserve a very grateful thank you."

"You have been kind enough Gloria, what else can you give me?"

"Something that I haven't given away for a long time, why don't we go somewhere for the weekend Gordon we can revive our wonderful past...I must say that, my divorce to John has shattered my life, I need someone to revive me...You know I still have loving feelings for you Gordon, please darling don't turn me down...."

"Well, you are the one who turned me down, you knew how mad I was about you, and yet you married John!"

"Yes you are right, and I am so sorry."

"And yet you went to Italy to see him, I guess there's something going on between the two of you!"

"Absolutely nothing's going on Gordon, I went to Italy to get some papers signed, also for the simple reason Suzanne and family were there, and finally he owed me some money, he has paid me back and on top he paid for my staying in his hotel, that was rather expensive, you can imagine a five stars with three swimming pools, Suzanne and I spent almost every day swimming, that's where she met Barry, that bloke who was in the restaurant with her last weekend!"

"Okay Gloria let's go somewhere nice then, shall we go to Cornwall, I heard from a friend of mine who spent a week in Padstow, he had a wonderful time!"

"Why not Gordon, how about next Saturday then we can comeback on Monday!"

"Lovely darling, I've been so miserable lately, I really need a break, maybe because I have been very busy,,,, **(Gloria put her arms around his neck and kisses him fondly, in that moment of bliss Suzanne enter the room without knocking)**

"So sorry Gloria, maybe I should have knocked, hello Gordon..how are you?"

"Very well thank you, and you Suzanne? Gloria tells me that you are over the moon about your fabulous venture, and says that you like my choice of colours."

"Yes I must admit you have done a fantastic job, I don't think anyone else could have done as good as you!"

"Thank you Suzanne, I do appreciate your words, I must admit, this business with you and Gloria it's going to be very successful, believe me!"

"Thank you so much Gordon......Anyway Gloria, the reason I popped around is to tell you that I've given my notice in, of course my boss was quite annoyed, more than anything upset, as he said, he'll have a problem replacing me, he ask me to work an extra week, on top of my week notice, how about that Gloria, have you set the date yet?"

"Well, say we shall be in full swing in three weeks time, is that alright with you Suzanne?"

That's fine with me Gloria, after all the work you done, I guess you need some rest yourself...!"

"As a matter of fact, Gordon and I will go to Cornwall for this weekend coming, you might as well know that handsome young man were engaged before your uncle showed up!"

"Poor old uncle I guess he will never have you back now!"

"You can say that again Suzanne, he has been a very naughty boy with me, but I have forgiven him, life is too short to bear grudges."

"Very true Gloria...Did you hear that Gordon? I really hope you'll enjoy you two.... and please don't do anything I wouldn't.... I'll give you a ring next week Gloria...Have a nice time..Bye!"

"She's a lovely girl that Suzanne, you know I still treat her as my niece, I hope she will marry Barry, they a wonderful couple."

"Actually I know his father, he built my friends' house, must admit he's a good builder!"

"Okay then Gordon, is that all set for Saturday? If so what time are we going to leave?"

"Say if we leave early morning, we can be down in Padstow late afternoon, right to have a freshen up and then go out for a nice dinner, how that's sound?"

"Perfect Gordon... say we leave at seven **am**...okay!"

"Right I'll pick you up at seven...."

"Oh I nearly forgot...here's the cheque for your wonderful work, my father is very satisfied with your price... and bytheway, just bear in mind that our weekend expense will be fifty, fifty"

"Thank you for the cheque Gloria, don't worry about the cost of our weekend, we haven't even left yet...Bye darling!"

"Bye, bye Gordon...see you on Saturday!"

(Same day....Back In Italy in John's chalet with Lucia, they were both having a nice drink after those pleasantly couple of hours., which were disturbed by his mobile phone)

"They just won't leave alone John, ah, ah, ah,..."

"I told Jean I was going to have a couple of hours rest, as I was up early.....Hello Jean...what is it?"

"Sorry to wake you Mr. Collins, you are wanted here at the reception, someone is querying his bill!"

"Alright darling, I'll be there in five minutes!"

"Is this Jean English then?"

"Yes she's from Kent, she's been in Italy for over ten years, she's a good dam worker, and much better than that lazy assistant manager I got, still I suppose I could not run the hotel on my own...!"

"What do you want me to do John?"

"Tell you what Lucia, just get dressed and go back to the pool...Later on I'll give you a lift back to your place!"

"Don't you want me to stay tonight, I want you so much!"

"I am very tempted Lucia, but supposing Luca changed his mind a he's coming back tonight!"

"I don't think he will darling, even so, I can always say that I spent the night in my parents' house, or even a trusted friend of mine Nina, she lives alone!"
"Listen I must go now, I'll see you back at the pool, alright darling?"
"As you wish John... I love you so much, and thank you for making me very happy..."
"See you later Lucia....."

(On his way to the reception John was thinking to himself all sorts of thoughts...."All I want now is to get caught with her, that'll be another big problem, and maybe he might even gun me down for sharing his wife, she's lovely though, and very sexy....But is she sincere? I'm getting very suspicious of all this, seems to me everything turned out so easy, I should have stuck with Gloria, she's not bad either, a bit demanding though!"

"Here I am Jean...let's have look.....that's it then.... cancel that.. and give him the new price with the discount, as we want him back again, we can't afford to lose customers!"
"If you say so Mr. Collins... thank you for coming, and so sorry to disturb you, I hope you had a nice relaxing time!"
(looking at him with a smile, as if she knew he had Lucia in there with him)

"You know something Jean, when you rung I just couldn't wake up, I felt like someone have given me some sleeping tablets, maybe I shouldn't get up too early in the morning!"
"That's probably the reason........ But I am not so sure about that!"
"Come on Jean... What do you think it is then!"
"Maybe you work too hard....ah, ah, ah, ah!"

"I sense a little sarcasm in that Jean...."

"Sorry Mr. Collins... Maybe I think you need a good massage!"

"You could be right Jean, is that an offer?"

"Maybe......? I think I better finish this bill!"

"I think you better Jean! In the meantime I shall go and make my usual checking, if everyone turned up for the second shift"

"Okay Mr. Collins...Take it easy!"

Chapter 28

(John became more worried, now he started thinking that Jean or someone else probably saw him with Lucia, and naturally started to reassure himself that he wasn't doing the right thing, so he said to himself, as much as he enjoyed the situation, he thought that he should find a way of stop it for the moment, but what about Lucia, she could get upset, thinking I used her for personal satisfaction, yes, so he approached her laying on that sun bed....

....As he looked at her laying there with sun glasses, wearing just a tiny bikini showing half of her bosoms......he thought;)

"Bloody hell.. she's beautiful, she's the best human creature I ever came across, come on John be strong and put yourself together......"

"Hello darling , did I wake you up?"

"No John, I was miles away!"

"I guess you were thinking about Luca, maybe is having a good time in Rome too!"

"Not really I was thinking about you...I just can't believe that you've been so nice to me!"   i

"I hope it was something more than nice..."

"More than that darling, I was thinking how gentle and soft your hands were when spam that cream over my body!"

"Come Lucia, you are exaggerating now, my ex wife always complained about my hands being too rough!"

"Your wife didn't have a good taste of the most beautiful things that a man possess!"

"Goodness me.. I never knew that we possess such beautiful things, would you mind telling what they are?"

"Not here silly boy, there's time and place for everything... do you think I could have a cold drink? I'm just melting away in this sun, in my garden it's not so hot!"

"have you got a big garden then and is it nice?"

"Not really...It could be nicer, if my lazy husband would look after it, instead is busy with other things!"

"Such as...?"

"Can't tell you John, not here anyway, even the flies have ears, believe me don't trust any creatures or human beings in life, the world is beautiful, but full of tricksters!"

"That's true, and your husband is one of them and that it's one of his nasty pleasure in life!"

"Yes John.... and I've got to live with it, this is why I want to spend the night in your harms tonight, one pleasure I haven't had for a long time!"

(The phone rung again..."Bloody hell I think I'm going to throw this phone in the pool!... Yes Jean... Okay I'll be there in a minute......Sorry Lucia, I must go up to the reception...I'll see you in ten minutes..."

(Soon after was back again with Lucia)
"Sorry Lucia, that was a false alarm, Jean there was something wrong with the computer, but quite common, it wasn't plug in correctly!"

"Don't worry John, I guess this Jean don't want you to be with me anymore for today, I hope you don't have an affair with her... never get involve with members of your staff, they could get you in trouble very easy!"

"Good lord Lucia, what makes you think that? Believe me I would never do such a thing, anyway Jean has got a boyfriend he comes an d pick her up every day!"

"That doesn't mean a thing...she's here all day long and many thing can happen in between!"

"Good lord you are suspicious, Lucia...come on then I'll take you home, we cannot risk our beautiful relation just for one night..Can we meet again tomorrow at the same coffee bar?"

"Why? What about if I come here at the pool again, then in the afternoon we can do the same thing again!"

"Yes..but if we have lunch together again, people will start thinking, you know darling..."

"Yes you have a point there, I think we better wait until Luca gets his job in Rome then we'll be free to see each other whenever we wish, I love you so much John, believe me, I really mean it, and this it's not infatuation either!"

"Come on then I will drive you home..."

"Don't worry John I have my car just parked down the road, but please you walk me over there if you like!"

"Of course I will darling, and please don't ring the hotel, if you want to speak to me, ring on my mobile!"

"You do the same John....I am ready if you are...."

"Here we are John, this is my rolls royce, I just love it, lovely fiat five hundred."

"I think my niece Suzanne has one of those... she said they are lovely cars!"

"Yes they John and very reliable, very easy to park!"

"Indeed very handy to park anywhere you like. look let us just shake hands, just in case some nosey parker sees us kissing, You never know there are some powerful camera nowdays.....thank you for the beautiful afternoon...see you soon darling..."

"Yes it's true.....Goodbye John and thank you so much...."

(Back in England, Suzanne was getting worried as she did not hear from Barry for the past few days, but as she was thinking..... her mobile rung...)

"Hello... Hi Barry, I was getting a bit worried about you I thought something had happened, how are you darling?"

"I'm okay thank you, are you well?"

"Yes I'm okay, I've just come back from Gloria, don't laugh, she was in the new salon with Gordon, and silly me I did not knock on the door, and there they were kissing each other!"

"I am not surprise Suzanne, I remember her telling me about this Gordon being her boyfriend once, actually when we were in Italy, I mean her and I at the pool, I think you went to see your uncle that time for something or other."

"Well..I was quite embarrassed, but I could see they were not, also she told me that this weekend they are going to Cornwall for three days!"

"Lucky them.. Suzanne I rung you because a friend of mine told me that tomorrow evening they are going discoing to a well known place, they also have a restaurant there where you can have dinner or a snack, which ever, what do you think? We haven' had a dance since our holiday."

"I'd love to, Barry, you know I've only been a couple of time to a disco, with some girls friends from school, that was a few years ago."

"Well, it'll be nice for you to see how upgraded the discos are now!"

"Shall I take my car this time, so you can have a drink?"

"Not really, I'll come and pick you up at seven, is that alright?"

"That's fine Barry...See you tomorrow at seven...bye.."

"Bye darling...bye..."

(Barry arrived at seven, Suzanne was ready, of course the parents warned her to be very careful, with her drinks, as there was some stories going around that fellows started to spike girls' drinks, quite interested to hear about that, and as soon she was in the car she mentioned it to Barry)

"Your parents are right Suzanne, I heard that too, I will make sure that whilst the two of us dance our friends will seat and look after the drinks."

"That's a good idea Barrie as my parents said that a couple of girls had to be taken to hospital, that's how bad the staff someone put in their drinks."

"They reckon they put some kind of drugs that really makes very sick...Bytheway Suzanne, I'll have to pick up my mate, as his car wouldn't start, he has an old banger, poor fellow, is such a nice mate, we went to school together...is name is George and she's Tina!"

"Hello George...hello Tina... This is Suzanne, my future wife....ah, ah, ah, ah"

"Steady on Barry, at this rate we'll have ten kids...Nice to meet you Tina and you George too..."

"Nice to meet you too Suzanne....Thank you for picking us up Barry, you know... I was telling Tina here that I must change that car, and look out for a second hand one a bit better!"

"It's your lucky day George, my father works in a garage where they have quite a few second hand cars, I bought mine there!"

"Many thanks Suzanne, perhaps later you can give me the address, and I'll pop over and meet your dad too."

"Of course George with pleasure..."

"Are you local Tina?"

"Yes I live just on the outskirts..."

"How lovely, what do you do Tina..."

"I help out in my uncle grocery shop, but I really like learn to be a hairdresser..."

"Well...that's my profession, in fact in a few weeks I shall open a new salon in Littlewood, I just employed an apprentice my next door neighbour's daughter, if we need another one would like me to let you know?"

"That would be fantastic Suzanne, I want so much to learn that trade..."

"Lovely don't forget to give your phone number..."

"Yes I will, thank you Suzanne!"

"Blamey Suzanne... you done your bit already this evening as a business woman."

"Thanks Barry...I'm always delighted when I can help someone, next I shall help you to do a new dance ah, ah,"

"See George? She's not only beautiful but also a good dancer...I'll look forward to that...."

(The evening went very smooth and no spiked drinks, Barry dropped George and Tina, who were grateful for the lift, and so phone numbers were exchanged. Barry arrived at Suzanne's house and....)

"Thank you Suzanne for the lovely evening I really enjoyed it, and of course the good company of my friends and yours now!"

"Thank you Barry, you are always so nice..."

"Please don't say another word Suzanne, I really love you so much, perhaps next week you must come for dinner at my house and your parents too!"

"Oh thank you Barry that'll be lovely...I will say nothing to my parents, when you'll invite us, I'll just surprise them, I'm sure they'll be delighted....**(Kissed each other with love tenderness)**

"Goodnight darling...sleep tight!"

"You too darling...I love you!"

(Back I Italy.....It was getting late for John, he thought all that womanizer business was getting on top of him, he thought he needed a break, he was now checking some account in his office, when Jean the receptionist popped in with a couple of letters for him to sign)

"Thank you Jean, I feel so bloody exhausted you wouldn't believe it!"

"Yes Mr. Collins, I understand how you feel, but I could suggest a remedy, that is if you don't mind........."

"Well, if it would do me any good ...why not?"

"I think to calm your nerves you should have a good massage, I used to be a masseuse you know?"

"Yes, I used to work for that Chinese firm in Flint street, then I got sack because I had more customers that the other girls!"

"Bloody hell, you must have been good then, mind you when I employed you it didn't show on yours curriculum!"
"True, I must be honest, it's because I used work in black....you know what I mean...."
You mean you used to dress up in black?"
"No...No.. I used to get paid in cash only..."
"Oh I get it.. I guess you used to do only massages."
"Well if anybody else wanted some extra special treatment, I would oblige, mind you I had my limits.."
"Okay then Jean, what time you finish tonight then?"
"Probably ten o clock!"
"Well then... I was thinking to have an early night, you can come down to my chalet and give me a good massage, that will get me in full swing for the next day, are using any special creams?"
"I've got them all Mr. Collins, you won't regretted!"

(Half past ten and Jean did not appear, so John had his nightcap of whisky, and jump into bed and thought: this will make me sleep alright!"
Just about to fall asleep when his door bell rung....)
"Who's is it?"
"It's me Lucia......"
"Okay just a moment...Good gracious Lucia...How did you get in?"
"Well... I got in from the main entrance..."
"Did anybody asked you...anything?"
"Not a word from anybody, actually the lady behind the reception was talking to a customer, as I walked through."
"You know something the lady, actually Jean in the reception is supposed to come here and give me a massage, as she was a masseuse before taking her job here..but she hasn't turned up, I was wondering why...?"

"Well, you might as well forget her....I'm here now, and I can give you a massage.... after all there's no arm in that"

"Oh no you won't, I think I'll walk you down the back entrance, and take you home..."

"Oh..... no you won't, I am here now and I will stay!"

"What about if Jean turns up...what am I going to say?"

"Just tell her you are so tired, you can't be bother to have it tonight...simple as that!"

"Well.. I suppose you are right, let me switch off the lights, then she'll believe that I was half asleep."

"Well thought darling...I feel very tired too, and I think I'm going to sleep...first let's have a cuddle, like my mum you to say!"

"Please do John....but be gentle.....Oh...You are a darling, I knew I could not leave you on your own tonight."

"You are just terrible...But I love you Lucia!"

"Me too John, please let me stay forever....."

Chapter 29

(Fortunately Jean never turned up, and John was quite happy, as usual he woke up just after six, had a shower and back he was in the reception, but before doing so he gave Lucia her marching orders, before the situation could get more complicated. John returned to his chalet few hours later, and Lucia was gone, he sighted with relief, and started thinking how...not so much of getting rid of her, but to work a simple way not to make their affair too visible to the hotel staff.
So... later in the afternoon Jean turned up for her shift.)

"Good afternoon Jean.. you know something last night I laid on the bed and before I knew it I went to sleep right away, only realized this morning that you didn't turned up, what happened?"

"We had quite a few late arrivals, and by the time I sorted all their documents, I thought it was too late...sorry about that.

"Not too worry Jean, I'm so glad that you care about your job, I think I shall have a word to Mr. Rocco to make you head of our reception, and that would mean more money in your pocket!"

"Thank Mr. Collins, I do appreciate that, my boy he'll be going to college soon and for that he will cost me more!"
"How old is your boy then?"
"Is sixteen, and thank god I do a bit of massages from home, that is a bit of a help!"
"I admire your dedication... keep on the good work Jean!"
"Thank you sir!"

(Late evening John gets a phone call from Lucia, and tells him that Luca is back from Rome, and is happy that he got the job he was offered, considering is problems with the law, she says he's a lucky man, first because his boss retrieved his accusations as it was a computer mistake, and to compensate him for that he gave him good references, for his new job)

"Yes John, the bastard is once again a very lucky man, and I am a very lucky woman, to know that he will start his new job in a few days, I have already told him that I want a divorce, he hasn't said yes yet, but he seems inclined to do so, as he said he's very happy to go to Rome!"
"That is wonderful Lucia, I'm sure you'll be better off without him!"
"Yes I will John, but I won't be very happy on my own, I want to be with you, because I truly love you!"
"I think we better sleep on it Lucia, first of all I want to see you completely free, then we can talk about marriage!"
"We don't have to get married John, we can still be happy living together!"

"That's true, as I went through one divorce, and quite honestly I don't want to go through another one, they are very expensive now days!"

"You are right John, but we'll see what the future will bring, I am so glad that I found you, and I don't want to lose you!"

"In the meantime Lucia let us take things easy, for a start you won't be able to come until he's gone, if he finds out you would lose everything you are entitle regarding your separation!"

"I know that John. Yes let us keep in touch only by phone!"

"That's alright, you ring me and make sure you don't leave your phone at his disposal!"

"Thank you, I will try and convince him that best solution is the divorce, as we haven't consumed our marriage for a long time, through his fault of course... I will let you know John."

"Thank you darling, make sure you don't leave hanging around that hotel Pass I gave you, that could a hot proof for him to get every penny out of you!"

"How about if I destroy it?"

"Please do that, you can always have another one!"

"Must go now John, I see him coming up the ally..bye!"

"Bye darling take care!"

(Couple of weeks went by, and back in Italy the new salon was about to open, Gloria and Suzanne were over the moon as it looked like the ones you see in Bond street London, very classy indeed and very affordable. The first week was a bit quite, but the second they found themselves quite booked up)

"Suzanne I think we'll have to employ another hairdresser and also another apprentice".

"I think you are right Gloria, I think I got another apprentice, and I might have another experienced girl, and that's the one I used to work with!"

"I don't want you to get yourself in trouble by taking away one of your ex boss's staff, what do you think?"

"Well, when I left she said; that she was looking for another hairdresser as my ex boss didn't pay her enough!"

"Then is another matter, if you know how much she's getting now, surely we can give a little bit more, why don't you ask to come and see us tomorrow?"

"I will, I'll ring Helen this evening, and I shall ring Tina too, she'll be over the moon to the job as an apprentice!"

"Good, if we can get them two, we'll be okay Suzanne!"

(Suzanne rung Helen and she seemed to be very interested, no problems for Tina, who said she could start the next day. Helen went to see Gloria and Suzanne two days later, and she agreed to accept the new job at "Suzanne's new hair salon)

"So glad you can join us Helen, I hope you didn't upset your boss too much by leaving."

"I don't think so Suzanne, maybe he was happy, as we were not all that busy, I think the problem is that he increased his prices a bit too much!"

"I understand that Helen, in times like these we have to be careful with prices!"

"All the told him that his tariffs were a bit to high, but he didn't care at all, I think he's rich enough...Okay then I shall give my notice in on Monday and I shall be with you the following one!"

""Just great Helen... we'll see you then...bye.."

(A week later Helen was at her new job a little bit early, Gloria and Suzanne gave her a few instructions, and an introduction to the two apprentices weren't to be missed too)

"Before we start girls I must tell you some good news, Barry has proposed to me, in fact there it is the proof..." **(showing her new engagement ring)**
"Oh I am so pleased for you Suzanne, as a matter of fact, I've got some good news too....Yes...Gordon asked me on Saturday just look at this..." **(showing her beautiful ring too)**
"My god what a beautiful day this is, may I be the first to congratulate you two?"
"Thank you Helen...Thank you Helen..."

(Suzanne was home a little bit late as they wanted to clear up the overbooks, mum Claire just finished to prepare the dinner)
"So glad you are so busy Suzanne and very happy that you managed to get two more staff, Helen is a nice girl and a very committed worker I saw her in the old shop how hard she worked!"
"Yes mum, and also Tina, she's good, and ver4y pleasant with the customers!"
"Well....girls, I've got some good news too, from next Monday, I'll be running the garage, today I interviewed a young chap who was working for the Hollins garage, and he has accepted to come and work for me, Jack will stand aside, mind you he said; he will give me a little help now and then, until I get myself in full swing!"

"That's wonderful dad, I am so pleased for you, and of course thanks to Jack is been very kind to you!"

"Yes, he has been very kind to me, he's almost given to me for nothing, good old Jack!"

"They really enjoyed their dinner when they came here a few weeks ago!"

"Yes they did Claire and he still talk about it, we must invite them again, they haven't got many friends and of no children either!"

"Does he have any relatives or brothers or sisters?"

"Not that I know Claire, still they seem to be quite happy!"

"Bytheway Eddy have you heard from your brother John?"

"No, I haven't heard from him for two or three weeks, last time he told me that he will pop over in September for a couple of weeks!"

"Is he coming on his own, or has he found a new companion?"

"Knowing him he probably found two companion!"

"He' quite a guy your brother, no matter what people say, I think he's a very good hearted!"

"Yes mum I like uncle John very much, and I think he should come to my wedding!"

"Did Barry mentioned the big day?"

"Not yet mum but he said that he will come and ask dad my hand!"

"I thought he would never do that....!"

"Of course he would dad...He mentioned that a few times, once he said, that you might turned him down!"

"Rubbish...He can have you any time...."

"That's not very nice Eddy!"

"I'm only joking Claire...only joking!"

"I think we should have a double wedding..."

"What do you mean mum?"

"Yes... You and Gloria..."

"That would be funny, not so much for my brother, as I think he still very fond of Gloria."

"Are sure dad....What make you say that?"

"I know my brother more than you do girl, I'll tell you that!"

"Come on then you two, eat up your pudding, I want to clear the table and go the other side to watch that new film!"

"Yes mum...I want to watch that too... for a start I shall take all these dishes in the kitchen..."

"You are a good girl really....One more thing I'd like to tell you Suzanne, you better start learning how to cook, as you don't want your husband to live on take-away!"

"True dad...I thought about, I think you should teach me mum."

"Of course I will darling, starting from this weekend!"

(Suzanne's gone in the kitchen)

"I think I shall ring my brother later Claire."

"Please do Eddy, I want to hear some gossip, good news for a change!"

"Tell you something Claire, if he wrote his life story, it would be a best seller...!"

"I believe that Eddy, I bet he had more hot dinners than us two..."

"Claire...mind your language, good job Suzanne is in the kitchen..."

"For goodness sake Eddy, I think she knows more about the facts of life than you and I put together......"

Chapter 30

(Couple of months gone by on the Italian Riviera, Lucia and Luca was now filling for their divorce which was mutual agreed, John was now nearly free to see her but they were still to be very careful, not to aggravate the situation, still, Luca was most of the time in Rome and nothing he could do as they both signed and it was going through as predicted.
And so they met at usual coffee bar in the afternoon)

"Hello darling, how are you today, have you heard from him then?"

"Yes, and the good news is that he told me that the divorce will be finalized sometimes next week, and then I'll be free as two birds, correction....me as a bird, him as a devil."

"You are a beautiful bird, I'm so happy darling, as soon that is done I will ask my boss...Mr. Rocco if we can live together in that chalet, until of course we can find our own place!"

"Oh...I am so happy John, I still can't believe that we shall be living together!"

"I wonder what your ex will say, when he'll find out!"

"I don't care, he can think or say what he likes, but the good thing is that I do not belong to him anymore!"

"He'll probably call me all the names under the sun for what I've done to him, on top of it I stole his wife!"

"You shouldn't worry about that John, he has done some bad things to you too!"

"Anyway, my brother rung me last night, some good news too, Suzanne is engaged to that Barry who was here on holiday few months ago, and my brother is got his own business now, repairing cars and he's doing rather well!"

"Oh, I am so happy for him and for his daughter. Do you think they'll invite us for the wedding?"

"I expect so, she's my only niece, and I love her very much, she's such a beautiful girl, when she was here on holiday, she was the star of the hotel."

"I'm looking forward to meet her John, and of course your part of the family...not to forget your mum and dad!"

"Plus another thing which I never told you, Suzanne she has opened with my ex wife a new hair salon, and they are doing so well that they had to employ more staff."

"But that's wonderful John, I hope you don't still have loving feelings for your ex-wife!"

"No way Lucia, when we parted we were both sad but in time we got over it, in fact when she was here on holiday, we were just good friends!"

"Why did she come here on holiday then?"

"First...Because I had to signed part of the house we were living in, then of course because she's very attached to Suzanne and knowing that she was here with her parents she thought to pay a visit to all!"

"Well, this family affairs, I mean family problems are never ending, I had my share too with my own family when I used to live in Florence, of course my parents are no longer with us, but I've a brother gallivanting here and there!"

"You mean you lost touch with him?"

"Unfortunately, or I should say fortunately, as I helped him out many time from his gambling habits, I don't really want to know that much, let him stay where he is."`

"I know the feeling Lucia....I must go back to the hotel, they probably wonder where I have gone!"

"Okay darling I see you later, what time do you want me over!"

"Come at nine so we can have some dinner together!"

"Bye, bye darling see you later..I love you!"

"Bye...love you too..."

(Back at the hotel John was talking to Jean)

"Everything alright Jean?

"No problems what so ever Mr. Collins, Mr. Rocco popped in for five minutes, he asked where you were, I told him that you popped out for half an hour, I asked if he had any messages, he said nothing that important and then he left!"

"I shall give him a ring later... Many thanks Jean!"

(John thought to give him a ring just in case, just in case more problems came on the horizon)

"Hello Mr. Rocco... sorry I missed you I had to go out for half an hour, did you want me for something?"

"Oh yes John, I wanted to ask you about that Luca, have you sorted out your problems!"

"Yes indeed, he turned out that, he also he was sacked from the last job, in a way I felt sorry for him, I told him that he should learn how to treat people in a decent way, times have changed since the end of second world war, let's take example of some of my staff!"

"Yes I know John, That receptionist of yours is excellent, what was her name again?"

"Jean, yes she's very reliable, some days she works extra hours without asking for more money...!"

"That's good John..Keep up the good work!"

"Oh Mr. Rocco next time you come over I would like to ask you something, this is actual very personal, I don't like to explain it on the phone, it's nothing serious but I would like to talk to you in private."

"But of course John, look I'll be over tomorrow afternoon, and you can tell me this secret of yours!"

"That's wonderful Mr. Rocco, in the meantime I would like to apologize to you when we had that disparity of conversation, I was a bit out of line...I think!"

"I don't think you were John, actually I like people who stand up to other people and themselves now and then, I don't like people crawling as to get something for nothing, and from now on I don't mind you addressing me as Rocco, forget the mister."

"Thank you but I don't mind to address you as mister, this is a matter of respect!"

"I do understand John, you do as you please, after all, apart from owing the hotel, I'm just as human as yourself!"

"Thank you Signor Rocco, this sounds better, I'll see you tomorrow then."

"You can count on that.....Now I'm curious to hear what you've got to say...Bye for now..."

"Bye, bye signor Rocco!"

(The next day Rocco arrives, as usual immaculately dressed in a grey suit and red tie, his little moustaches made him quite important amongst other people and without failing to say hello to any of the staff that he encountered)

"Good afternoon Jean.. Is Mr. Collins around?"
"Yes sir, he's in his office, would you like me to call him?"
"Thank you Jean, I shall go and see him myself!"
(Knock, knock..." Can I come in John...?"
"Of course sir, the door is open..."
"Here I am at you disposition John, please tell me!"
"Well... You know that problem with Luca?
"Yes....Go on..."
"After you left I rung his home number and his wife answered, her name is Lucia. Did you ever meet her?"
"Never..."
"I told her the money problem I had with Luca, she told me that she knew nothing about that, and she told me that that was nothing new, Luca always had problems, however to cut a long story short, the next day she came to see me, I tell you something, what a woman, elegant, sophisticated, well mannered, and really, really beautiful, and on top of it she handed over an envelope containing four grand and she said that she would give me the other two soon."
"I can't believe that....go on..."
"I said to her not to come here at the hotel, if anything I would prefer to meet somewhere, so we met in a coffee bar, that's where she gave the other two grand, she told me all her problems and she was planning to divorce him...I asked her out for a chat and a coffee.. again and again and we fell in love.....**(and so John kept on and on)** as now they are divorced, we are planning to buy our own place, but in the meantime, could she come and live with me in my chalet?"
"But of course John, that's no problems at all!"

"I thought for using the chalet, she would be willing to help out in the kitchen or restaurant when needed, without pay."

"That is not fair John, if she works here she must be paid, as you are my manager the living in goes with it!"

"Thank you Signor Rocco, we are planning to get married soon, and for certain you'll be invited to the wedding!"

"Thank you very much, and I'm looking forward to meet your future bride!"

"The other thing is that very soon I'll be taking two weeks holiday, I would like to go and see my parents in England, sadly they are getting old.. I am sure my assistant will be able to cope, after all we Jean now she's very good keeping half of the staff in line.."

"I am sure the hotel will be okay, after all I don't think we shall have the amount of residents soon!"

"Yes unfortunately, the season is dying down a bit, but we are still doing very well!"

"So I can see from the takings, keep it going John and good luck with Lucia."

"Thank you signor Rocco, I really do appreciate your kindness!"

"Don't worry John, my kindness is nothing in compare to Luca's, in the end you got your money back plus his lovely wife, so, keep on smiling....I must leave you now, I've a business man to meet...see you soon John!"

"Bye, bye Signor Rocco and thank you again!"

(John thought to ring Lucia and tell her the good news)

"Oh..I'm so happy to hear that John, so now as soon as Luca will pick up his belongings, I shall have to put the house on the market, then we can look around for a better one..."

"And make sure you don't leave any money hidden away!"

"I think he probably emptied his couple of safes....Last time he was here , I saw him messing about in them!"

"Okay then Lucia, start picking up a few things, then you can move in my chalet, I said to my boss, that you will help us to run the Hotel, I'll find a couple little jobs for you to keep you occupied! Although he said there's no need for that, at the same time he likes to pay you too, for any work you will do!"

"That's wonderful John, I don't mind at all, I worked in a hotel before, as a receptionist, I can replace Jean when she has a day off!"

"Good...then you will help out Jean, as she's always very busy. Anyway when you move in I shall introduce you to all the staff, so they will know who you are!"

"That's wonderful John... Thank you...See you later."

"See you later darling..."

Chapter 31

(Back in England a month later Gloria and Suzanne was closing up the salon, after a very busy day)

"Before you go home Susanne I would like to let into a secret, which only my parents know about!"
"Let me guess Gloria... two things, whether you are pregnant or you are getting married."
"You guessed the second one.. yes we have fixed the date, and it will be in eight weeks."
"Congratulations darling, I bet you decided when you went down to Cornwall!"
"No, only a couple of days ago... Yes we had such a wonderful time in Cornwall, we didn't know that we were made for each other....Yes Suzanne we are in love."
"I am so glad for you Gloria..."
"Well...you know..... We enjoy immensely being together, unlike John it was a normal thing..... with Gordon is different, yes he makes me feel a new person!"
"You lucky so and so....probaly my uncle took you for granted"
"How about Barry...do you....you know what I mean...?"
"No we are saving it for our wedding day, he did make a few little advances, I just told him to be patient!"

"I think you should let yourself go a bit more, do you love him Suzanne or is it just an infatuation?"

"Yes I do I love him, sometimes I miss him when he's not around!"

"Well then.... you see, but you've got to be both very careful, make sure you don't go to the alter with a big belly!"

"No chance of that Gloria...Bytheway, I think uncle John he's visiting us in a couple of weeks and his bringing his new girlfriend, I think they'll be staying with his parents."

"Nice to hear that, good chance for him to see our new salon, after all it was partly his idea!"

"I didn't know that Gloria!"

"Of course his idea came when he thought about you, he thinks the world of you!"

"You are right Gloria...yes I think the world of him as well as I always wanted to meet someone like him, but there's only one uncle John..so I got myself Barry, who's very nice really, he'd do anything for me, he really loves me!"

"So make sure you don't lose him, otherwise you'll be sorry one day."

"Say no more Gloria, I got your point!"

"This evening we'll sit down and make a list of the invitations..."

"Don't forget me Gloria..ah, ah, ah, ah!"

"Of course not darling, I can't afford to do that, where would I find another Suzanne?"

"Thank you Gloria...see you tomorrow..."

"Bye, bye Suzanne... say hello to Barry for me!"

"I will...bye, bye..."

(Two weeks later. John and Lucia were arriving at the airport, and Eddy was going to pick them up)

"There he is my big brother....Hello Eddy....how are you brother? Bytheway... this Lucia my future bride..."
"Nice to meet you Lucia..."
"Nice to meet you too Eddy... John I'd like to go to the ladies, please before we get in the car!"
"Of course darling...is down there on the left, we'll wait here!"
"I say.. you've got a good taste, she's really beautiful."
"Thank you Eddy...she's a lovely girl, I told you she just divorce her husband, he was the manager before at the hotel, and he was a bastard with the staff and a tyrant with his wife too, I made sure he paid a good price for his doings!"
"You didn't kill him John?"
"Not really...here she comes, don't mention her husband!"
"I won't John.... Okay Lucia?"
"Yes thank you Eddy....
"Right.... here we go to Greatstone, bytheway, this evening you two, mum and dad will come to us for dinner, Claire has been busy all day long, you know what she's like!"
"That'll be nice Eddy, if you stop at the super market I will buy a couple of bottles of wine."
"Don't be silly John, I bought a case of Chateauneauf du pape this morning."
"Bytheway, congratulations, how's your new business?"
"I'm doing alright John, in fact I had to employ another mechanic, Jack has been very nice to me, mind you he's quite happy now, he deserve all the rest he can get!"
"You know Eddy, he could have sold that for a lot of money."

"I don't think they need a lot of money, they have no children, no relatives..."

"I wouldn't be surprise he'll leave everything to a charity."

"He might do, in the meantime, he likes to see me running it.. here we are at home sweet home of our good parents.. we'll see you all at seven, I think dad will drive you...see you later!"

"Thanks Eddy bye..."

(Dinner at Eddy & Claire's house)

"Hello darling Claire, how are you? Look at you with your multicolour apron, I can see you've been busy!"

"Hello brother in law, and who's this beautiful lady then?"

"May I introduce you to my future bride? This is Lucia, she doesn't speak a lot of English, but she manages okay!"

"Nice to meet you Lucia, please sit down.."

"And this is my beautiful niece Suzanne..."**(Approaching her and giving her a hug and a kiss)**

"Hello Suzanne, your uncle talked a lot about you!"

"I hope something nice Lucia!"

"Right then let us have a good drink before dinner....

(And so they drunk and they dined to a superb meal, mixing with a lot of news from Italy)

"Yes, we live in my chalet at the moment, just waiting for Lucia's house to be sold, then we shall look around for a place of our own!"

"Are you getting married again uncle?"

"Of course darling, and pretty quick, before someone else steal this beautiful girl!"

"Why not John, it's about time you get your head in one place and stay there!"

"Your dad is right John, you are not getting any younger!"

"Of course mum, this is going to be forever...Oh dad do you think I can borrow your car these few days so I can take Lucia to see some places? Also I would like to pop in to see the new salon, and say hello to my ex...if you don't mind Lucia!"

"Of course darling, you do that, but I'll be watching you!"

"See what I mean Eddy? I'm already being watched!"

"Nothing unusual when you are almost married John..."

"Come on then you lot, let's move to the other side, and I shall bring the coffee, in the meantime Eddy ask them if they want a liqueur or a brandy!"

"Right Oh...Mrs. Collins...!

"Uncle why don't you come up tomorrow to see us, I look forward to show you how nice it is!"

"Yes I will is that alright eleven in the morning?"

"That's fine uncle... I don't know if you have heard that Gloria's getting married in a few weeks!"

"Yes your dad told me in the car, why not, she can't stay spinster all her life, she deserve a good husband!"

"I'm so glad that you still friends you two!"

"Why not Suzanne, life is too short to bear grudges, then of course... we did settle the misconduct amicably!"

"Yes it's true uncle, that 's the best thing!"

"This is a lovely bedroom they gave us your parents John, and that was a lovely evening John, your families are so hospitable, they really know how-to make you feel at home!"

Thank you darling, yes they are, pity my brother had only one child, I would have liked a couple of boys too!"

"Suzanne is very nice... I think I notice something very strange about her, sorry not so much strange, because it is quite normal in humans..I hope you don't mind me say so!"

"By all means darling..what was it?"

"Well.. I noticed when you kissed her, she blushed and she hugged you with closed eyes, as she seemed to find pleasure doing so, don't misunderstand me, I think you ought to know that in my teen I felt that way too about my uncle too, he was over twenty, much older than me!"

"I don't believe that darling, surely I would notice anything like that!"

"You probably would if you see her as different girl, but as you are her uncle, you might not even think or feel such behaviour!"

"I find your observation quite impossible, alright she might like me or love me, but as an uncle..I think..."

"That's what you think, I'm sure you heard stories of students falling in love with the teachers!"

"Yes I did, but I still find hard to believe what you say!"

"Alright sweetheart...don't worry no one will take you away from me!"

"Thank you darling, nice to hear that I have a beautiful bodyguard now!"

"You can count on that darling..."

"Right I'm going to wash my teeth, and off we go dreaming!"

"Only after you done you duty.....ah, ah, ah, ah!"

(John went off to the bathroom, looked himself in the mirror and thought: "Bloody woman she doesn't miss anything, fancy finding that out about Suzanne, I hope I don't speak in my sleep"

"Oh... that was a good wash...bytheway darling, I thought you were speaking in your sleep last night, do I do that too?"

"I don't think you do darling...you sleep like a log!"

(John thought)...Thank god for that."

(Next morning at the breakfast table)

"This what I call breakfast mum, the Italian don't have anything like this, all they eat in the morning..brioche, fruits and toast and off course coffee, not have tea...But when lunch time comes they make up for it, big plates of pasta!"

"A good breakfast gives strength all day long, do you agree John?"

"Yes I do mum..."

"Me too, after a hard night....I mean after too much food and drink the night before!"

(Lucia and John looked at each other and laughing)

"Go on son go and say hello to your ex...and Lucia keep an eye on him..."

"Thank you Anne I shall keep my both eyes on him, rest assure about that!"

"Take care of my car John....!

"I will dad... I will, bytheway mum, don't bother cooking tonight, I think we are going down the road to have a pub meal! And tomorrow evening we'll take you all out to a nice restaurant, so don't make any plans you two."

"Don't worry John, very unlikely we'll make any plans at our age!"

"See you later mum...dad...ah, ah, ah, ah!"

"So this is Littlewood John, what a lovely village and quite big I'd say!"

"Oh yes, it was very small once, now look at it, it's like a small town, I used to come to high school here, this were I met Gloria!"

"So you were school lovers then...some memories...!"

"Yes some memories all gone in smoke! mind you I must tell you that there was another admirer of Gloria, and I think is the one she going to marry, my brother said that his name is Gordon, I don't really remember anyone of that name to honestly... Still, that is in the past and now here we are facing the present.... I haven't done too bad meeting you..... Have I?"!"

"I would say you won at the lottery....ah, ah, ah, ah!"

"Hello...Hello...Gloria this is heaven, what a beautiful place... I am so glad for you and Suzanne of course!"

"Thank you uncle... Gloria would like to meet your future bride!"

"So sorry Gloria... this is Lucia, and yes she will be my future bride...if she still wants me!"

"Don't worry uncle, you shouldn't' worry about finding other girls..."

"OH.. I say Suzanne that a good compliment....Nice to meet you Gloria, I totally love your salon... and please don't take any notice of him, you should know what he's like! He's always full of compliments."

"No need to tell me darling, I still have nightmares!"

"Thank you Gloria..I thought we remained friends!"

"Of course we are softy, you are still my number one school mate! Go and sit in the waiting room, Tracy will make you a coffee, and we shall join you, Helen.... can take over for half an hour."

"Of curse Gloria... leave that to me..."

"Thank you we'd love a coffee."

(Lots of good news were exchanged between the four and most of all Gloria invited John and Lucia for her wedding)

"So nice of you Gloria, but I doubt very much if we'd be able to come, Lucia is selling her house then we must look for another, time is very precious with my job, the hotel is nearly full all the time, actually we were hoping to spend two weeks here, but we shall stay only one."

"I understand John, but before you leave Gordon would like very much to meet you and Lucia too, perhaps the two of you can come to mum and dad and we can have dinner there!"

"First ask your mum and dad, tonight and tomorrow we are busy, maybe the next day, not much time after that, please let us know, further more how do they feel your parents having me and Lucia for dinner?"

"Don't be silly, you know very well, that they will be pleased to see you no matter what happened in the past, it's water under the bridge now....!Oh in fact Suzanne you can come too, if you are free that evening!"

"Thank you Gloria I'd love too, I haven't had much time to be with my favourite uncle!"

"You haven't any choice, Suzanne since John is your only uncle, anyway I understand you saw him a lot when you where in Italy, John told me that you were at the swimming pool every days!"

"That's true Lucia, I was there because I wanted to be with Barry...He's my boyfriend now...You know?"

"Yes I know darling..take care of him, I understand he's a nice boy...There are very few around these days!"

"I think we are a bit late to see those two people in Greatstone Lucia...so we must make a move...Thank you for the coffee Gloria... I am so please that you have a good business here and you Suzanne."

"Thank you for coming and it nice to meet you too Lucia, look after that lucky devil of yours now!"

"I will Gloria, don't worry... come on you get in that car..."

"See..what I mean Gloria...?..Bye darling you just take care, I will let you know about the dinner!"

"I will give the message to Suzanne...bye, bye....!"

"Lovely people John, especially your ex... she's a lovely girl...Did you notice anything about Suzanne?"

"Come on Lucia...give it a break, I don't think she is the way you think she is..."

"Alright John for goodness sake at least let me say that she's infatuated to a point that she would do anything to get what she wants, but of that is impossible because she's your niece and please forget what I said, I'm sorry...very sorry if I offended you!"

"Darling don't worry, I am not offended, I do accept your criticism and I am pleased to know that she loves me as a dear old uncle!"

"I'm sure you are, so keep your distance, you might think I'm jealous...Yes I am, because I love you!"

"And I love you too darling!"

(The fat Duck, was a very old pub, in the centre of Great stone, and John just wanted Lucia to try their true English cooking)

"Look Lucia you must try that pie and mush with green peas with bacon and onions, it's lovely, I always have that when I come here!"

"Okay the then... Pie and mush it is, and I I'll have a glass of white wine."

"I'll have the same darling, but I'll have a pint of Ale...!

"What's Ale ?"

"It's pure English old beer, lovely when you are thirsty..Look who's coming in..."

"Oh it's Suzanne and that must be her boy friend Barry."

"Yes it is...Hello Barry...hello Suzanne...."

"Fancy meeting you here uncle...hello Lucia...!"

"Hello Barry..Please meet my future wife Lucia..!"

"So nice to meet you Lucia, I guess you are from the Riviera..!"

"Yes I am Barry, but I don't think you saw me at the hotel, my ex husband was working there ...You know?"

"Was he the one with moustaches and not very tall?"

"Yes unfortunately that was him, why were you there a year ago?"

"Yes I have been there with my parents for the past three years!"

"So you remember my ex husband then? What did you think of him?"

"Not a very pleasant fellow, if I may say so, rather abrupt most of the times, I remember him telling the workers to get on with their duty and not to keep talking to the customers!"

"Yes he was like that Barry, Must go the ladies to freshen up John, do you mind?"

"That's okay darling... Come on you two sit down with us, what would you like to drink...?"

"Thank you John, I shall go to the Bar and get them myself, the same for you Suzanne?"

"Yes please darling.........Oh finally I can talk to you uncle, I missed you so much, you have no idea."

"Look Suzanne this has to stop, I must tell you that Lucia realized that you... you know....?"

"How does she know that uncle?"

"I just don't know Suzanne, maybe it's just a woman's intuition..."

"I can't believe that uncle...I love you so much, I can't stop thinking of you!"

"But Suzanne you have the boyfriend now, and you got to stick with him."

"I don't know uncle I feel so confused, even when I kiss him, I think of you, because if I don't think of you I don't feel anything about him!"

"Look darling, there's nothing you and I can do, it' s quite an impossible situation, and believe me it's the way you talk to me that Lucia knows your feelings, because the same thing happened to her when she was your age, she fell in love with her uncle too!"

"I understand uncle, I suppose I'll have to try and forget what happened between us, but you'll be always in my heart, I love you so much!"

"Good girl...watch it Lucia's coming and so Barry with his drinks, keep smiling as if nothing has been said...."

"Hello you two.. what have you been talking about?"

"I was just saying to Suzanne how beautiful it's the new salon, and I am so pleased that Gloria has given Suzanne's name on the entrance....really looks super!"

"Yes it does John, super and beautiful as you niece...my compliments Suzanne and you are so lucky that you have a very handsome boyfriend...just don't lose him, he's going to be the most precious person in your life!"

"Thank you Lucia for your good words ... I just ask my uncle and you if you can invite us to your wedding!"

"Of course my dear, you and Barry are most welcomed and all your parents!"

"Did you hear that Barry? We are invited to their wedding, I just can't wait"

"Provided you will come to our wedding too Lucia..."

"Do you really mean that Barry?"

"Of course I do...first I must make an appointment with you father to ask your hand, I don't want him to think that I'm stealing his daughter and ask for a ransom !"

" You are so funny Barry......My father he's free anytime Oh..I love you so much..."

"That's what I like to hear darling, and I love you too!"

"So let's drink to that then...Cheers....Cheers....!"

(The chat went on and on so much that the famous bell sounded the closing time, like it used to be in the old times)

"You know Barry I haven't heard a bell ringing for a long time in pubs!"

"Neither did I John.....Mind you I can't say that I frequent pubs a lots as I live on coca cola!"

"Better than getting drunk on whisky, my dear boy!"

"True John...God lord you sound just like my father, bytheway, my parents they send they regards to you both, and they said they were looking forward to meet your future wife...."

"You tell them that we shall pop in to say hello before our departure!"

"I will don't worry.......Cheers to everyone and thank you for your lovely company... Would you like a lift John?"

"No thank you Barry, as it is a nice evening I think we have a pleasant walk, my parents don't live very far!"

"Goodnight all...and see soon..."

(And so the two happy couple left the Fat Duck smiling and looking forward for a bright future)

(John ad Lucia holiday break has finally has come to an end. Sad time for everyone to see them leaving but John had to fulfil is obligation and responsibility to his job and to his new future wife, sadly they won't be able to attend Gloria and Gordon's wedding, but they were equally happy to have met Gordon the night before at a dinner party celebration at Gloria's parents, everyone was there and it was a super evening. So, departure day arrived for John and Lucia and a very sad day for Suzanne who hid a few tears from John, Barry lovingly kept his arms around her, promising to attend their forthcoming wedding.

The hotel staff welcomed them back with joy and wishing them a very happy future.......)

"Some other publications by the same Author available on Amazon"

"Love and Champagne"	Published	June 27	2019
"The lonely, lonely Clown	Published	July 9	2019
"Music the food of love	Published	September 21	2019
"Julian's Angels 1	Published	January 4	2020
"Julian's Angels 2	Published	June 19	2020
"Julian's Angels 3	Published	October 29	2020
"I was an Alien"	Published	June 28	2020
"Princess Snowdrop"	Published	February 16	2021
"The Roman scarecrow" 1	Published	April 2	2021
"The Roman scarecrow"	Published	August 26	2021
"Mr. World"	Published	November 30	2021

©"A family love affair"
Words approx; 60.700

Printed in Great Britain
by Amazon